Soul

Sessions

Carson

This edition published by
Dog Ear Publishing
4010 W. 86th Street, Ste H
Indianapolis, IN 46268

www.dogearpublishing.net

ISBN: 978-145753-404-1
This book is printed on acid-free paper.

Printed in the United States of America

This is for all the people who've unfailingly helped me ...
far too many times to count. Many of you did so without
realizing the impact of your kindness.

Wolverine Weekend

"You're a piece of shit," Janice screamed as her angry hand smacked flush across my face, three times in rapid succession. Her wild tirade was a startling wake-up from an early evening nap. More vengeful words spewed from her before she turned and stormed out, leaving the front door to my condo wide open. This was punishment for an indiscretion committed weeks before. I don't know how she found out, but what does it matter? In the grand scheme of things, Janice is the least of my problems.

For the next eight hours, I clutched my pillow and felt smothered by heavy darkness that was crushing me to the point that I couldn't take a deep breath. I had no energy and was unable to climb out of bed, even to just walk to the bathroom.

Alternating my gaze between the clock and the bottle of pills to its right, I wondered how many gulps of a densely packed Ambien-vodka cocktail it would take to end the suffering. The green neon clock indicated 2:17 AM, and as each minute rolled into the next, my mind raced like an out-of-control Indy car weaving in and out of traffic.

I was trapped in a feeling of relentless fear. *But fear of what?* I'd do anything to make it stop and knew going to sleep would be the highlight of my night.

Soul Sessions

Six months before, I'd started to show signs of depression after a freak plane crash in Atlanta had killed all one hundred twenty-seven passengers and crew. The plane had barely gotten airborne before "technical difficulties" crippled the engines, causing the plane to crash. I'd been traveling on business and was ticketed for that flight. Ultimately, only a two-hour traffic jam on I-85 in downtown Atlanta had kept me from being one of the unfortunate passengers.

Once the reality of a brush with death had set in, I'd become so shaken that I canceled my later flight and rented a car to drive the twelve hours to Chicago. I haven't been the same since.

It's become a nightmare that won't leave my mind. I've started to fly again, so it's not a fear of flying or dying that's been driving my sadness. Unable to put my finger on why, I've felt overwhelming disillusionment as depression has been crawling under the bed sheets to join me for nights of endless tossing and turning.

Suddenly, awakened by a firm tug on my shoulder, I realized it was morning, as the sun was just beginning to peer through the heavy wooden blinds. It was Janice. _She's back already?_ We were dating and didn't live together, but I'd foolishly given her a key to my condo. She must have staggered in after the late-night clubs closed down.

Ugh, she was giving off that awful smell of a perfumed ashtray. She'd told me that she had quit smoking, but it was obvious she'd been lighting up. Janice was still in her mini red dress from the night before, and her hair was a tangled, Medusa-like mess. She must have crashed on the couch.

Janice held my cell phone in her outstretched hand and nudged my shoulder again. "Nick, wake your ass up. I answered your phone. It's Jeffrey from college. I told him you're awake. By the way, I'm still pissed at you."

She was always suspiciously snooping through my phone and occasionally picking it up and answering on my behalf. I decided to put a passcode on later that day.

Jeffrey Harris is my former college roommate from Michigan, whom I hadn't seen much since our graduation fifteen years before.

No doubt Jeffrey could hear Janice's comments, but chose not to acknowledge the situation. "Nicky, my man, long time no talk," he said.

We exchanged the usual chitchat and then Jeffrey got to the reason for his call.

"You gotta come to Ann Arbor next weekend and see the Wolverines put a beatdown on Michigan State. We're gonna spank their Sparty asses and make them cry like little girls. Everyone from the old crew is coming. I've already got hotel rooms and will get us great seats. All you need to do is say yes and show up. So get your pretty-boy ass in gear and let's do this shit," he said.

It was somewhat jolting to hear how upbeat Jeffrey's distantly familiar voice sounded, given my state of mind. He'd always been the life of the party in college. I remembered him as a tall, pudgy type with a blonde crew cut, a Chris Farley type. Jeffrey tended to be loud and boisterous, often bordering on obnoxious, but damn, he was fun.

During our senior year, he got so drunk at one of our parties, he opened the oven door and threw up in it. He neglected to tell anyone. We only realized it two days later when we started cooking a pizza. The smoke from the burning vomit on the bottom of the oven consumed our entire apartment and triggered a visit from the fire department. I guessed Jeffrey hadn't changed a bit.

As I sat up in my bed, thoughts of how exhausting it would be to drive the two hundred forty miles from Chicago to Ann Arbor crossed my mind. Even the limited sex I had these days was exhausting. The demons in my head were just getting started on all the reasons why not going was the preferable alternative. *How had things gone so wrong?*

My thin veneer of quiet confidence, occasionally bordering on smug had vanished. Before the depression struck, my mind was never suffocated by negative thoughts. Perhaps a college football weekend with old friends was just what I needed, I thought, as I consciously tried to beat back the invisible demons.

With all the energy I could muster, I put on a happy mask. "Okay, okay, I'm in. I can't wait to see you jackasses."

Clearly excited, Jeffrey said, "Fuck yeah. Now that's what I'm talking about, Nick. This is gonna be sooooo epic. Damn, I hope I get laid!"

I was curious to see how everyone had changed. Fifteen years can do a lot to a person. I hadn't changed physically all that much, I suppose ... still in good shape, possessing considerable height, and relatively good-looking with a full head of straight black hair always combed neatly to the right. The inside was a different story though. My outlook on life had evolved drastically, and certainly not for the better.

I'd had substantial career and personal success, but for the past several months, a nagging feeling had persisted. Something was missing in my life. Like everyone, I'd had ups and downs, but this was different. In an invisible fog and feeling empty, I knew I'd slipped into a deep depression that was becoming harder and harder to control.

It was a mysterious and continuous aching that had infected the very core of my being. I'd been craving the idea of stepping out of my life ... stepping out of what I called "The Darkness" ... the way one steps out of a cold, damp winter night into a fire-lit home.

Throughout the week, I went back and forth as to whether I'd actually go on the weekend binge. I wanted to see my old college friends, but the thought of having to put on a happy face all weekend felt dreadful. It had been getting harder to just get out of bed and gear up for work. Each day had become a ritual of gathering up my willpower in the morning to begin the process of trying to fool everyone into thinking all was well. The self pump-up process was taking longer each day that went by.

By Thursday, I'd contrived an excuse to cancel on Jeffrey. Just as I was minutes away from calling him to deliver the disappointing news, my cell phone began buzzing.

"My man. It's Jeffrey. Just letting you know, I got us tickets on the fifty yard line, fifteen rows up. Damn, I love StubHub. I'm pumped. You ready to blow it out?"

"Ummm ... ya know ... work is crazy right now, Jeffrey."

"Perfect! Even more reason to come party it up. Can't wait to see you. By the way, I'm your wing man this weekend, not that dork Roy. I'll ride your coattails like old times. Oh my God, we're gonna get laid! All right. Gotta go. Have a call coming in. See you tomorrow night, mo fo."

Throughout much of their lives, Roy and Jeffrey had struggled at getting attention from women. I remembered Roy as a tall, thin string bean with greasy hair. He had a ridiculous overbite and always tried to play the nice guy with the ladies. He was warmhearted to the core and had an obsession with disco music that I never quite understood.

In college, our group had a game we played called The Burden. Basically, the way it worked was one guy in the group carried The Burden until he got laid. Once relieved of The Burden, he would pick another member of the group to pass it on to. Poor Roy. He carried The Burden our entire junior year. Jeffrey carried it for six months during our sophomore year. No doubt, after a few weeks, The Burden began to weigh heavy. I had The Burden once, for less than a day. In retrospect, perhaps I took the game a little too seriously. Once The Burden had been passed to me, I'd gone down a mental Rolodex of every girl I'd slept with at Michigan, until Shelley, an impressionable, fun-loving Little Sister to our frat had come through with a timely "yes."

On Friday night, we gathered in Ann Arbor at our favorite old hangout to drink, reminisce about old times, and catch up on what we'd been doing the past several years.

Contemporary rock blared as Jeffrey, Eric, and I rolled into the bar like we owned the place. Damn, it felt good to be back in a town with so many unforgettable memories. The scene was how I'd remembered it, except everyone looked so much younger. *Had college girls really looked this young when we were in school?*

The walls were covered with past Michigan sports glories and the wood floors were permanently soaked with dried beer. God, I missed that smell. The bar was still dimly lit by neon beer signs, while the ample number of flat screen TVs scattered throughout the bar were a nice addition.

Throughout the evening, members of our crew started to arrive. By nine o'clock, all eight of us were gathered around two dart boards, playing team cricket, wagering twenty bucks a game. We'd all aged so differently. Several hairlines had receded. Jeffrey had put on another forty pounds, while a few of us had stayed in pretty good shape.

Our life trajectories had gone in completely different directions. Eric was married with two girls, while others in our group also had kids. Despite all of our varied challenges, everyone seemed to be doing well. Even Roy was smiles, despite his recent divorce. *Was I the only one hating life, infected with a severe case of wretched emptiness?*

After another half dozen Hoegaardens and more remember-when conversations, I confided in Jeffrey and Eric my feelings of emptiness and lack of fulfillment, although I held back sharing my thoughts of suicide. The dart games had ended, and many in our group had already gone back to the hotel a half mile away. Jeffrey, Eric, and I remained at the bar.

Eric is the one friend among the group whom I've remained in contact with since college, mainly because he lives in Oak Brook, an upscale suburb twenty miles from my downtown Chicago high-rise. However, work and life had kept us from seeing much of each other lately. Truth is, I was avoiding him just like everyone else in my life.

Eric commented that I didn't seem to be my usual hard-driving, hard-partying self, although initially, neither he nor Jeffrey took what I was hinting at seriously. Naturally, Jeffrey steered the conversation toward women.

When asked, I said, "Sure, my girlfriend, Janice, is great to look at, but our relationship is going nowhere. We don't have much of a connection; we just pretend that we do. I certainly don't love her."

Janice is a 5'10" buxom thirty-one-year-old brunette. She's the kind of woman who walks down the street and turns heads. Although conscious of her good-looks, she never acknowledges the double-takes, looking straight ahead through the Prada sunglasses she regularly wears, even on a cloudy day. She has the power to look right through you.

Sometimes I've felt like the latest in a long line of successful, handsome men she's dated, although most have been a good bit older than me. She's easily charmed by money and a man's man who puts her in her place. No doubt my manliness score has taken a hit since Atlanta.

When we're out, she loves to have a girly drink in one hand and a Bella menthol filtered cigarette dangling in the other, irrespective of whether smoking is allowed in the club. Her "game" is to try to appear mysterious and unattainable, although, she has the depth of a kiddy pool.

For the past several years, Janice has "worked" at Jimmy Choo's, an ultra-upscale shoe store. Ironically, she's found that Choo's has been an ideal venue to meet men of her liking. She works ten days a month or so and travels the rest of the time.

Sometimes she's joined me on business trips when the destination has been of interest to her. She likes to spend her time shopping and being pampered in the hotel spa while I'm in meetings during the daytime.

At night, she's typically come along to client dinners, making perfect eye candy for the dinner participants. She can be a lot of fun, and definitely adds some spice to the boring business dinner scene. Janice likes to alternate her tease, sometimes showing off her ample cleavage with low-cut tops ... accentuated by a Y necklace that hovers just above the parting of her natural double D's. Other times, she spotlights her long, muscular legs with five-inch heels. Part of her allure is to show one asset while leaving other charms to one's imagination.

In addition to traveling with me, she takes a lot of "girl trips" to Vegas, Miami, and New York, where who knows what or who she's been doing. My guess is they've not all been "girls trips," and I'm certain she's not been faithful.

I suppose my secret vice is being seen with a long, sultry woman like Janice. If I'm honest with myself, it makes me feel good for all the wrong reasons. I know other men look at me and think, *You lucky bastard, you get to bang her as often as you like.*

And as far as other women go, I actually find it easier to attract women for future encounters when I'm with a strikingly beautiful woman like Janice. I'm the first to admit in the eighteen months we've been dating, I've not been faithful to her. Guilt is not a condition from which I suffer.

"What about your career? Nick Dalton, big investment banking partner, making a ton of money. Sounds awesome to me," said Eric.

I ordered a second round of shots and noticed I'd been pounding the Hoegaardens faster as our group had thinned out. "Sure, it sounds awesome, Eric, but actually it sucks. I'm totally unfulfilled by the work. Advising CEOs on buying and selling their companies is intellectually stimulating, but it's also a lot of disingenuous salesmanship and cutthroat negotiating. It's not what I thought it would be. Honestly, I feel handcuffed by the money and am pretty miserable."

Meanwhile, Jeffrey was eagerly waving at us to join him at a neighboring table with some rather young-looking co-eds. We ignored him as Eric shared a story of how his wife, Caryn, had had similar feelings of emptiness a few years back. He described Caryn's depression as severe, to the point where he nearly had to have her hospitalized.

After chugging his remaining half bottle of beer, Eric said, "Nick, get a professional opinion. I'll text you the info for Caryn's former therapist when we get back to Chicago. Caryn said she's Ivy League-educated and well thought of, although I have to forewarn you, she's quirky and unorthodox. But you'll like her. Oh and make sure you never throw a plastic bottle in the garbage around her. She's nutso about the environment."

Undeterred from our earlier indifference, Jeffrey coaxed the three girls over to our table. Trailing them, he caught my eye and mouthed a silent "just go with it." To say the conversation that followed was ridiculous would be an insult to the word ridiculous. "Ladies, these are my teammates Nick and Eric. As I said, they're from the ninety-seven national championship team. Of course, Nick played for the Dallas Cowboys and just retired, ya know."

The girls seemed reasonably impressed and clearly knew nothing about football. Eric and I were amused at first, and played along with Jeffrey's ruse for another fifteen minutes or so, but, much to his disappointment, we put a stop to the comedy shortly after last call.

Feeling pretty buzzed, we bid the girls a good night and started walking back to the hotel on a crisp, chilly night. Neon signs were being turned off throughout the strip of bars, while inside, waitresses lifted overturned barstools onto tables. "Go Big Blue" and "Sparty Sucks" occasionally rang out from the people roaming the streets at two AM. For the first time that fall, we could see our breath as we continued walking and talking about women, getting older, and how weird it felt to be back in Ann Arbor.

The rest of the weekend was fairly uneventful. Michigan won 28 to 24 on a late touchdown pass that had 110,000 fans at Michigan Stadium in a frenzy. The Darkness was largely kept at bay, although throughout my time in Ann

Arbor, I had a strange, almost eerie feeling that somehow, my depression had something to do with my days at Michigan. The sense was palpable, particularly when we were at the game.

Sunday morning at breakfast, we went through the obligatory comments about how we needed to do a better job of staying in touch, promised to get together again next year, and then said our goodbyes. Eric reminded me he'd be sending a text.

Shortly after returning to Chicago, The Darkness re-awoke, as it had been lurking just under the surface all along. For the next week, I kept looking at Eric's text containing the contact information for the therapist he'd suggested: "Dr. Katrina DuMont … DO IT BRO."

Another week passed and more questions swirled in my head. Incessant internal chatter kept coming back. *I'm lost. Why do I feel something is missing? Why can't I seem to get excited about anything? Why am I having trouble sleeping?*

I feared the night ahead … another night jailed under the covers with an invisible nemesis … another night without restful sleep.

Surviving Katrina

I reluctantly decided to reach out to Katrina DuMont's office and set an appointment. After some back-and-forth calls, we set a ninety-minute meeting for the following Saturday, in the afternoon. As the day to see her drew closer, I found myself anxious, uncertain, and looking for a reason to cancel.

At the last minute on Saturday, knowing I needed help, I found myself at Katrina's before I could back out. Her office was located on the second floor of an old two-story building in the Lincoln Park neighborhood of Chicago. She had a small unattended waiting area which was kept dimly lit. The room had a heavy Eastern influence, decorated with Buddha statues, yin-and-yang tapestries, and a small fountain that offered the soothing sound of moving water. The worn dark brown hardwood floor was covered with a thick patterned Persian rug that felt as soft as pillows to walk on.

As I studied my surroundings, I couldn't help but wonder what was in store for me. My inner voice was carrying on a debate whether seeing a psychotherapist would be a complete waste of time or not. I felt a sense of desperation, tinged with a sliver of hope ... akin to what a gambling addict must feel when he's lost all his savings and is down to his last hand of blackjack.

Katrina emerged from behind the door. "You must be Nick. Please come in and have a seat on the couch," she said with a hint of French accent.

Notepad in hand, she pulled up a chair and was facing just a few feet in front of me, legs crossed. I found it odd how close her chair was in proximity to my seat on the couch. I leaned back to create a more comfortable distance.

As my eyes fell on her, I noticed she was in her mid-forties, tall, perhaps 5'8", and fit, with shoulder-length amber-brown hair. Her face was very defined and angular, with high cheekbones. Her skin was youthful for her age, as if she'd hardly ever been tanning. I found her pleasant to look at. She wore little to no makeup. She radiated an inviting demeanor and seemed to be permanently wearing a smile, even when she talked, as if she didn't have a care in the world. She was exactly as Eric had described her.

Out of habit, I noticed she was not wearing a ring. She caught me glancing at her hand, but didn't acknowledge it. She wore comfortable jeans, a stylish black sweater, and a necklace that strung together several prominent oval shaped gems. Each were red-river in color, accentuated with gold veins indiscriminately running through each stone.

When she was looking down at her notepad, I couldn't help myself as I surveyed her entire body. She definitely kept herself in good shape, likely into fitness of some sort. I could tell she had modest sized breasts under her sweater.

"So tell me, Nick, why did you schedule an appointment with me?" she said with an inquisitive tone.

I shared with her the range of emotions I'd been feeling recently and my personal situation regarding work, finances, relationships, and so on. We talked about that day in Atlanta and how it had seemed to trigger some deep-seated, disruptive emotions.

Additionally, we started to scratch the surface of several aspects of my life from childhood to the present. Much of the discussion centered on my love life in the past few years and my utter inability to restrain my taste for beautiful women.

I was surprised at how quickly I felt at ease with her, enough to reveal my innermost world. I said, "I'm not proud of my philanderings. And truth be told, I've had nearly a dozen failed relationships."

We went on to discuss how I'm still on good terms with many of my former girlfriends. I shared with Katrina that my relationships have typically evolved into one of two types.

Some of my former flames are what I describe as "erotic friendships," where we keep in touch, share what's happening in our lives, and occasionally hook up for a night of naughtiness. It doesn't really seem to matter whether either of us is in a committed relationship with anyone else; sex just happens from time to time. We share the forbidden vice of being enticed more by betrayal than by fidelity.

The second type of relationship has typically morphed into regular friendship where we keep in touch via text or phone and occasionally go out for drinks. Friendly and erotic conversation is the norm, but we've outgrown being together sexually. Of course, there are the few that I'll likely never see again.

Katrina was taking copious notes. She asked, "Why so many breakups?"

I looked away to avoid eye contact and to gather my thoughts. "I like meeting new women. There's a certain 'aliveness' that comes with it … you know … in the early days. I love the anticipation of getting naked and being intimate with a woman the first time … the aliveness of it all. It's a turn-on and a sweet intoxication that I crave. I'll admit it. But then the novelty wears off after a while and it starts to feel a little bit like work."

Katrina caught my gaze and without a shred of hesitation asked, "Nick, do you think you have an addiction to conquering different women? Some might call it sport fucking."

Hearing the graphic nature of the term coming from the lips of a woman caught me off guard. I expect it from my guy friends, but from her, I found the term distasteful and not representative of my situation.

Unsure how to react, I instinctively feigned shock and mild insult. She was unmoved and I realized this would likely get me nowhere. I cleared my throat and awkwardly swallowed a gulp of water from the bottle I'd brought and said, "I don't view women as sex objects, if that's what you mean. In fact, it's quite the opposite. I'm spellbound by their femininity, charm, uniqueness. I find women intoxicating in a good way, Katrina. I know what I've been doing isn't working. In the end, it's been unfulfilling. But if it's an addiction, then it's similar to being addicted to eating vegetables. I mean ... what guy wouldn't want to be in the company of beautiful women on a regular basis? It's a good thing, isn't it?"

I noticed Katrina sit up in her chair. Smiling, she gave a somewhat sarcastic chuckle. "Interesting point of view, Nick, particularly the vegetable comparison. That's certainly original, I'll give you points for that."

She stopped jotting down notes. Peering up and to the right, she twirled her stylish black reading glasses in her left hand. "Nick, you mentioned aliveness a couple of times. I'd like to explore that more."

"As I said, I'm not proud of it, but I feel more alive when I've just met a new and interesting woman. I'm filled with yearning, with excitement. It's a stimulus, especially when I feel an emotional connection and intimacy with her. And then the exhilaration wears off ... sometimes after a month, sometimes after a year. Once the exhilaration wears off, I'm unable to suppress my taste for other women."

She paused for a moment and looked at me with inquisitive eyes, seemingly pondering my lack of fulfillment. "Have you ever considered the possibility that your female pursuits are just false replacements for *true* feelings of inner aliveness ... or connectedness with your *true* essence?"

"Honestly Katrina, I'm not even sure what that means," I said, adjusting my position on the couch, trying to get more comfortable. *False substitutes? Connectedness? What the hell is she talking about?*

Seeing the resistance on my face, Katrina explained, "Some people have a sense of emptiness but have no idea what's lacking in their lives, so they look for external stimulus such as workaholic hours, drugs, addictive relationships, or forbidden sex. They become addicted to the stimulus without even knowing it. What's missing is an authentic connection with the inner self … connection with the soul."

I avoided direct eye contact for a few moments, mentally defending myself against her words, knowing she was probably right. In my discomfort, I looked at the clock and saw our ninety minute session was winding down. It had felt more like twenty minutes.

Over the next several weeks, Katrina and I spent our time together exploring my history of initially getting very excited about a new relationship and then losing interest within a matter of months. The conversations were interesting, but I wasn't seeing much of a point to them.

We also talked about my recent thoughts of suicide. "Katrina, I feel like I'm drowning," I said one day, "frantically treading water with every bit of energy I have to avoid sinking into an abyss. On most days, at some point I've consciously wanted to die. Somehow, I find the will to trudge on, but I'm tired … so damn tired of worrying about how my life is one struggle after another. Each time The Darkness wakes, I transform into a scared stranger in my own body … as if I'm not me."

Shoulders slumped, looking at the floor, I told her, "I've taken all of my aggression and turned it inward, so much, that I just want to go away. I call it my selfish wish. I know my parents would be devastated, although I'm not sure anyone else would really care."

We discussed how my negative thoughts were like ocean waves coming in one after another with no possible end in sight … to the point where I've largely surrendered my appetite for living. Work had become my only point of refuge and way of passing time.

"I know I work insane hours," I continued, "which puts strain on my personal relationships. It's one of the reasons I have Janice accompany me on some business trips. It hasn't helped, though. We're as far apart as ever, and the sad thing is, I don't really care that we're not any closer. We both know we're in the relationship for selfish reasons."

I confirmed Katrina's suspicion that I rarely felt connected with any of the women I was with. Kelly, an intriguing woman I had dated just before I met Janice, told me several times I was emotionally distant. She had said she never really knew me, the real me, despite countless conversations and intimate encounters. It was the main reason we broke up.

Kelly was the most goodhearted, genuine women I'd been with in recent years. I'd let her go without a fight, and at the time, all I had felt was a false sense of relief that I was starting fresh again.

Katrina and I spent the next several weeks conducting traditional therapy sessions, exploring my psychological make-up and exploring my human frailties. I was beginning to feel more and more frustrated and had grown tired of taking the anti-depressants I'd started before engaging Katrina.

Finally, after I'd been seeing her for a few months, I said, "Honestly, I'm not sure where this is headed. It seems like when I talk with you, I feel better for a little while, but nothing fundamental is changing. It's like a warm shower. It feels great for a brief period, but ultimately, it wears off pretty quick. I'm suffering inside but clinging to the hope that a breakthrough is coming.

"I know it's early on, Katrina, but I'm feeling a sense of despair. I'm fighting to hold my demons at bay, but I know it's just a matter of time before I'm lying in bed, looking at the Ambien and vodka again."

Katrina leaned forward and seemed to nod in agreement. I suspect she noticed a change in my eyes, something she'd likely seen before and recognized as desperation. "The

Darkness, its engulfing me. I can feel myself trying to run from it ... as if I'm no longer welcome in my own body."

She sat in silence for an uncomfortable period. I could see she was in deep thought, as if in a mild trance. Once she came out of it, she waited to catch my gaze and said, "Nick, I've been considering recommending a different approach, adding something highly unconventional to our sessions. It's called regression therapy and involves hypnosis."

She said she didn't know if this would work for me, but with other clients, she'd used regression therapy with some success.

"In the last couple of months, I've come to the conclusion you have serious psychological blockages that are causing your depression and feelings of emptiness. I don't think talk therapy and antidepressants are the answer for you anymore. With your permission, I'd like to more aggressively explore the possibility that past trauma is the root of your blockages."

I asked her how regression therapy works and she explained, "While you're in a highly relaxed or hypnotic state, you'll visually review past experiences that have meaning to your current situation. Through the heightened sense of hypnosis, you'll be able to recall details from your subconscious mind that your conscious mind doesn't recall."

Apparently, the practice is well established for many different purposes. For example, to enhance their investigations, the FBI and big-city police departments successfully use hypnosis to help witnesses recall untainted memories of license plate numbers and crime scene details.

"As you go deeper within, you'll uncover psychological blockages that are influencing you today. We'll conduct the bulk of the therapy while you're still under hypnosis. Essentially, we'll review what you are seeing … and why, among thousands of memories, you picked these ones to review. I'll guide you through a series of relaxation exercises. Once you're relaxed, I'll ask you questions. You'll remember everything, but I'll record each session for you to review later if you'd like."

Katrina went on to share that an acknowledged shortfall of traditional therapy is its focus on repairing a person's damaged ego. Regression therapy is an approach that could help me learn to rise above my ego and see life though a completely different lens. She suggested it might bring a fresh and radically different perspective.

Katrina put her eyes on me as she spoke with a serious tone, "Let's face it, Nick: Up to this point, your entire life has been ego-driven, focused on accumulating money, achieving career success, and sleeping with women who make you feel good about yourself. Over the last few weeks, I've come to the conclusion your ego isn't in need of repair."

I cringed inside and glanced away, knowing all too well my ego had not been lacking, except of course since the Atlanta plane crash.

She went on to say, "I believe your ego is preventing you from truly living in the present moment and enjoying your life. You're stuck in your conditioning. We're going to search within to understand the real you. You have no sense of perspective, no clear view of your true essence. Your entire life has been viewed from a false perspective. This is what's lacking in your life. It's as if you've been sleepwalking through life and don't know it."

She has a unique way of delivering tough messages, all while smiling, but her body language and eye contact indicated a clear sense of purpose.

Knowing this, I continued to avoid eye contact, silently resisting her words. *Sure, I'm depressed, but so are a lot of people. That doesn't mean I've been sleepwalking through my life.*

After receiving no response, she continued, "So, during our next session, let's begin a series of regression therapy sessions. If we do this right, each one will lead you to relive key aspects of your past memories. Ideally, we want to reveal new insights, new learning's, new questions ... and most importantly, view your life from a different perspective. All of which could be highly relevant to your depressed state of mind."

Katrina sat up in her chair, leaned forward, and pointed the reading glasses dangling off her fingertips right at me. "Nick, I have to forewarn you, this could take us places you can't currently conceive. Places that are murky and far away from your current belief system. Time is up for today, but I have some ideas on how to help you. It may involve you doing some things that are uncomfortable and unnatural for you."

Playground Hero

Perhaps it's the obsessive type A planner in me, but to ensure I'd be able to physically relax and quiet my mind at the regression, I instigated a completely draining, marathon sex session with Janice as the sun was coming up. Two intense rounds followed.

Sweat was pouring off my forehead when I climbed off Janice and rolled to the side, desperately downing an entire bottle of water sitting bedside. My chest was completely drenched from pressing flesh to flesh against Janice's equally sweaty chest. My heart was beating a hundred miles an hour and I could barely catch my breath.

Staring at Janice as her weak-kneed legs stepped into the living room, I couldn't help but think what an amazingly stacked body she had, despite seeing her naked hundreds of times. By her own admission, Janice is a "tough nut to crack," as orgasms don't come as easy to her as others I've been with. To ensure the right outcome, our sex had become unusually aggressive, filled with spanking, naughtiness, and her favorite bullet vibrator throughout. Janice is particularly turned on by dirty talk, which involves us verbally detailing each of our naughtiest unfulfilled fantasies.

Much to her frustration, this was the first time we'd had raw, thunderous sex in weeks, as my depression had tamed my normally voracious sex drive to a trickle. I felt a renewed sense of vigor.

After recovering from the sex session with Janice, I went on a five-mile jog along Lake Michigan. The morning air was cool and dreary, with a biting wind. Fallen leaves carpeted the jogging path. I was alone with my thoughts, as foot and bike traffic were largely non-existent compared to the bustle of summertime days. I hadn't been this hopeful since before my troubles had started in Atlanta.

I arrived at my usual Saturday afternoon appointment with Katrina physically drained, not knowing what to expect. I'd never been hypnotized before, and Katrina's words "dark and far away" seemed rather intriguing, yet troubling.

She started the session with, "Okay, let's pick up where we left off last week. I believe it's possible you've been sleepwalking through life on autopilot and don't even know it. Let's explore that proposition with an open mind. Can you do that?"

Instinctively, I didn't agree with the autopilot theory, but I promised to be open-minded.

Katrina explained that conducting a regression session was a fairly simple exercise. She asked me to take my shoes off, lie down, and get comfortable on her unusually long, heavily padded brown leather couch. Under my fingertips, I could feel that the seat cushions were covered with a white sheet that was jersey knit, like the inside of a sweat suit. My heart was beating faster than normal as I clenched the soft cotton and anticipated what was about to come. My anxiety was running high.

I felt my body begin to sink into the couch, as the cushions partially formed around me. Katrina smiled as she propped up my head with a pillow and covered me with a thin royal blue blanket. It offered a soft feel, the kind you want to snuggle up with on a cold winter night. I closed my eyes and tried to relax. The room was warm, in contrast to the gloom outside.

Katrina took her usual position in her chair a few feet from me, turned on an audio recorder, and began to walk me through a relaxation exercise. I like the way she takes charge. "Nick, whatever comes into your mind, don't analyze it, just try to experience it, even if it seems bizarre."

We started with a breathing exercise where I imagined breathing in beautiful energy and breathing out all of my stress. After a few minutes of focusing on my breathing, we progressed into full-body relaxation.

She guided me to relax my neck and shoulder muscles, my back muscles, my torso and legs, all while breathing fully. I imagined a golden light above the crown of my head bringing relaxation.

"Relaxing deeper and deeper. Imagine the light coming into your body, illuminating your head ... the light liquefying and streaming down into the body, touching every muscle ... growing more and more relaxed."

Katrina instructed me to imagine the liquid light completely surrounding my entire body, forming a protective cocoon. "In a moment, when I count down from ten to one, go so deep that your mind is not subject to the usual limitations of human memory, so deep that you can recall every experience you've had. Ten ... nine ... eight. Going deeper with each number. Seven ... six ... five. Feeling light and breezy. Four ... three. Deeper. Two ... one."

I expected to be resistant to any attempts to slow down my mind, but I could feel my body moving from a normal waking state to a highly relaxed state. *Perhaps it was the energy drain from my morning erotica with Janice?*

As Katrina would later explain, my brain waves slowed from a routine twenty-two cycles per second to a hypnotic six cycles per second. As my neck muscles reached a totally relaxed state, my head became unusually heavy and fell deeper into the pillow than I'd ever experienced. Warmth saturated my body. I could feel the *aliveness* in my arms and legs. It was a curious feeling.

While I was in this alert state of calm, Katrina guided me to imagine myself walking into a garden bursting with life, still surrounded by golden light. "Continue to open the deepest levels of your mind. You can remember everything. To show you this, let's go back in time. In a moment, when I count down from five to one, let yourself recall a childhood memory. Let the memory come into complete focus when I get to the number one. Five … four. Coming more and more into focus. Three … two … one."

Katrina tapped my forehead lightly. "Be there with the memory, paying attention to the details you are seeing."

Within thirty seconds or so, an image of a little boy on a playground came into my mind's eye. I began to talk softly but with deliberate purpose.

I'm three years old. I'm climbing up a large green slide at a park near my childhood home in Flint. The steps are metal, and there are metal rails to hold onto when climbing up the steps. I'm afraid, yet excited. It's the first time I'm climbing this high by myself.

The hypnotic state was similar to the feeling one has a couple of minutes after hitting the morning snooze button

... in neither a deep sleep nor a waking state. I continued to talk softly, uninterrupted.

I can see my mom below, watching me climb. With each step, I'm a little more scared, yet excited. Looking down two steps from the top of the slide, I'm way up high. My hands are squeezing the rails tightly, holding on for dear life. The rails don't go all the way to the top. They end with one step to go. It's an awkward transition to let go of the rails and try to position my full body onto the top step. It's too scary to stand up on the top step without holding onto something. A blanket of fear is covering me as I hang fifteen feet in the air, paralyzed with indecision.

God, those rails are cold on my little hands. My fingers are feeling painfully numb from the cold metal ... so numb it hurts. I don't want to climb back down. I'm up so high.

Reaching deep within, I shove aside any remaining doubts and let go of the rails to grab the top step, slowly maneuvering my body upward. My little legs are shaking, and I feel my right foot begin to lose its grip, as thoughts of falling create a flash flood in my mind.

After a brief struggle, I regain my footing. "Almost there," I tell myself. I maneuver my torso onto the top step and contort my body around so my feet are in front.

I can hear my mother cheering me on below, offering words of encouragement. Oh my god, I'm so excited.

Taking in huge gulps of air, my senses from the perch on top of the slide are heightened like never before.

It's a frosty fall afternoon. The wind is brisk as leaves rain down off the large oak trees with each wind gust. The red, yellow, and bright orange leaves blanket the ground. I can see an entire landscape beyond the playground. Parked in the distance is our family's only car, a beat-up rusty Chevy station wagon that dad is continually having to tune up. Memories of riding in that car momentarily fill my mind.

Everything looks so different from the heights of the slide. I feel the same sense of pride a mountain climber must feel after reaching a difficult summit.

Below, my mom has amped up her excitement, hopping up and down, yelling and clapping at me to come down the slide. God, she looks so young at age twenty-seven. I'd forgotten how beautiful and unweathered her look was in her twenties.

She's wearing her favorite tight-fitting red coat that she'd bought new earlier that fall. Mom doesn't have many new things to wear. Her white boots and matching white beret on top were both acquired at local garage sales.

I grab the side of the slide and start my rapid descent. It's a tube slide that goes around three hundred sixty degrees. In the last five feet, the tube opens up. It's the most excitement I've ever had. The four-second burst down the slide seems like minutes. I come shooting out of the tube at a slight angle toward the end of the slide.

Mom is there to catch me into her arms. She's laughing and hugging me, telling me I'm her little hero and how proud she is of me. I'm laughing as well, waving my arms and looking rather uncoordinated as I turn to run back toward the steps. All fear is gone now. I go up and down that slide at least another dozen times.

I couldn't help but smile as I remembered the moment ... all the love, the warmth, the safety of it all. Up to this moment, I'd completely forgotten about that day in the park with mom. Sadly, it was one of the few moments of pure bliss we shared together in my childhood. I suppose it was our high-water mark together ... peaked at age three.

Katrina whispered, "Okay, now hover above the scene. Try to understand the importance of the memory to you now. Why among the thousands of memories did you pick this one?"

With an almost supernatural ease, insights began to flow into my consciousness, as if directed from a more intelligent source, one I'd never experienced before. I continued to share with Katrina what my quiet mind was experiencing.

Since that moment on the playground, I've had a craving for achievement and success in the traditional sense. I grew up in a home where achievement was lauded, something to be worshiped ... blue-collar parents living vicariously through me. I achieved exceptional grades in high school and college, at the expense of developing a healthy and well-rounded social life.

Insights continued. Over the years, I developed social skills focused on getting ahead. I learned to be the master of so-called "vertical" relationships, with bosses and subordinates. I developed into a pleaser and successfully managed up and down the chain of command. I became extraordinarily gifted at spotting who could be helpful to my career and who could not. I managed people below me to achieve rapid and exceptional results, all assuring career success.

However, my social skills only partially developed for my close relationships, particularly so-called "parallel" relationships with peers, friends, and women. I mastered the art of appearing knowledgeable and interesting. I can certainly hold court and be the life of a dinner party, talking intelligently on a wide range of topics from world affairs to politics to all of the major sports.

But I'm unable to feel true intimacy, particularly with women. I excel at the initial stages of attraction and building a relationship up to the point of true emotional *intimacy. Erotic friendships are my preferred relationship. Then the pattern repeats itself and I become the master of emotional avoidance. I create false intimacy. I've done this with every woman I've dated since college.*

My work life has been extraordinary, filled with one amazing accomplishment after another. However, my love life has been rather ordinary, at best, filled with superficial and empty relationships with beautiful women. It's been a fruitless search for fulfillment that has no chance of success due to my inability to open up and experience true intimacy. I'm charmed more by novelty and naughtiness than by authenticity and fidelity. It's a sad reality.

My friendships have repeated the same pattern as my romantic encounters, mostly comprised of relationships based on convenience, originated through some connection with work. Of course, I have friends. Lots of friends. But none are particularly close. I keep them at a comfortable distance, again mastering emotional avoidance and false intimacy. None would say I'm their best friend. Come to think of it, it's rather sad to say that not a single person in the world would say I'm their best friend.

Katrina softly asked, "What importance is this knowledge to you now?"

More unique insights emerged. *That day on the playground was the first time in my young life I'd accomplished something significant on my own. My ambition involved overcoming a fear of heights and the ice-cold metal handrails. I'd been rewarded with zealous praise by my mom.*

In the hours that followed, she shared with everyone she crossed paths with what her little hero had done. I was in heaven. Since that moment thirty-three years ago in my hometown of Flint, without consciously realizing it, I've been chasing praise, chasing achievement, and chasing affection from women. This was a significant revelation, I thought, as insights continued to flow into my still hypnotized mind.

I realized it's the affection my mother gave me on that day and then later withheld for much of my childhood, due to her pursuit of molding the "perfect" child. The bar was set at perfection, no matter what the activity, whether it be school, athletics, or girlfriends. Anything short of perfection resulted in my perception of love withheld and emotional abandonment.

My numerous seductions in adult life have all ultimately ended in abandonment, whether it was me forcing the others to break up or me finding a friendly way to walk away. Each time, I ended up alone, to repeat the process all over again. Sleeping with an ample number of sexy women and then subsequently morphing the relationship to something less intimate has been a dysfunction that has defined much of my adult life.

My failed relationship with Kelly, a former girlfriend, was particularly telling, as she was a keeper by anyone's standards. In the end, I simply couldn't give her authentic intimacy. When Kelly broke things off, her sad eyes told me all I needed to know. She was lonelier in a relationship with me than when she was alone.

Images stopped coming into my mind's eye. After a long pause, Katrina whispered, "Good, Nick. Soon, it will be time to return to full waking consciousness. Let's rejoin your body in the garden, feeling yourself back in your body. Counting up from one to ten, you will slowly awaken. One … two … three. Gently waking up. Four … five … six. Feeling alive. Seven … eight … nine … ten."

The wisdom that had naturally "flowed in" was not of my creation. Upon awakening, I was blown away by what had happened. I looked at the clock. It indicated that more than two hours had elapsed. Katrina saw me glance at the clock. "It's a common experience for time to speed up while in a highly relaxed state."

I couldn't believe the crispness and clarity of the experience. I had been able to feel the cold in my hands from the slide. The other fascinating aspect of the experience was the clarity and ease with which the learning had come into view.

With a mix of excitement and confusion, I asked, "Where the hell did that unbelievable level of insight just come from? I've never experienced such clarity of thought."

Katrina smiled and suggested that the process of hypnotherapy coupled with guided suggestion had taken me into a state of deep relaxation and in a highly relaxed state, it had become easier for me to tune in to memories from another part of my consciousness.

"We don't have time to go into it right now, but just know your conscious mind represents only one aspect of your authentic self. During the next set of sessions and therapy to come, we'll be delving into the secrets housed in your subconscious mind and your superconscious mind," she explained.

Of course, I know a little bit about the conscious and subconscious minds, but what the heck is a superconscious mind? I wondered.

"Nick, we're just getting started. Over the next few weeks, we're going to develop a depth of self-understanding that you can't even begin to comprehend right now. I do want to reiterate, though, you may not like what you find. Sometimes you have to go through a cold, murky winter before there is a spring. Today was a happy childhood memory, but not everything we will see will be so pleasant."

Why is she so insistent on warning me about cold and murky places?

"One last thought for today: Over the coming weeks, I'd like to explore your tendency to focus on achievement, wealth creation, and the need to impress others. It seems as though you 'attach' your level of happiness to these outcomes. 'Detachment from outcome' is a concept I suspect we will be exploring a good bit further. In fact, we may find more insights into your life's purpose by delving deeper into this behavior pattern."

I walked out of her office unable to wait for next week's session. Work suddenly seemed secondary. When I arrived back at my condo, I felt totally energized for the first time since meeting Katrina. I felt hope. I wanted hope as much as a drowning man wanted air.

Damn, it felt good to be alive for the first time in a long time. I decided to text Eric. The Darkness was in full hibernation.

> *Drinks tomorrow night? How about Paris Club?*
> *Want to pick your brain about Katrina.*

A few minutes later, he texted back.

You finally decided to call her!!! Awesome.
Tomorrow works. Let's do 7ish. See you there.

Moments later, Janice came strolling in from one of her many shopping ventures, carrying an armful of overstuffed bags from the most expensive stores on the Magnificent Mile. She had the look of a celebrity, completely proud of herself for being a VIP pampered shopper. I wondered how much this was going to cost me.

"Hey, babe. Didn't expect you to come back over today. I just had the most amazing experience with my therapist. I can't wait to tell you about it," I shared with her.

Eyes rolling, she said, "I'm still pissed at you, Nick. And another thing … I don't really know why you pay to see her to begin with. It's not really something I want to hear about. It's boring. Really fucking boring, babe. Besides, I need to show you all the great shopping I did. I found some naughty thong bikinis for my trip to Miami. I need to go try them on first, and then we can eat … and I don't want to hear about any psychobabble talk."

Following the stimulating, seemingly endless, bikini modeling session, dinner was a disaster. Listening to Janice carry on about mindless reality shows for forty-five minutes was sheer and utter torture. *Who gives a shit about which shallow and neurotic woman the bachelor didn't give a rose to this week?* Despite the amazing sex we have, I'm starting to get over her plastic lack of depth, I thought.

The next day, Eric and I met at the swanky Paris Club in downtown Chicago. I requested a quiet booth with some privacy in the back corner, where we could safely discuss sensitive topics.

Eric was all smiles as he entered the bar. "Nick, hope my suggestion of seeing Katrina wasn't a waste of time."

"No, after a slow start, it's getting pretty damn interesting. I've got some questions I want to ask, though. If I'm prying too much into your private stuff, just say so."

"No worries. What do you want to know?"

I knew Eric's marriage to Caryn had been troubled a few years back. I had always viewed her as somewhat bitchy but hadn't seen her in quite a while.

"What led Caryn to go see Katrina ... and how did things work out? I'm curious to know what she experienced."

"Honestly, Nick, I don't know all the details. Caryn was pretty screwed up and terribly depressed. Katrina would record many of their sessions. Caryn still occasionally listens to some of them. After a few months with Katrina, it felt like she was a different person. Caryn is still evasive and private when it comes to her treatment, though."

"Did Caryn ever talk about going to 'murky and far-away' places ... of things not appearing as they really are in those sessions?"

"Hmmm ... odd that you mention that. Caryn's depression was pretty awful, so I'm not sure if what I am about to say has any applicability for you or not, but when I said she's a different person today, there are some personality traits that did a complete U-turn. You know how fucking nuts she used to get when she was stressed."

When I nodded, he continued, "She doesn't like to talk about it, but she did comment once something like, 'When you've seen some of the dark stuff I've seen with Katrina, my life is a cakewalk now.'"

Sweet Home Alabama

The next evening at dinner, when I brought up with Janice my revelations about the roots of my emotional avoidance and my insights on vertical and parallel relationships, she seemed more interested in lecturing the waiter for her steak being cooked too long and the slight wobble of the table when she leaned on it. I couldn't help but be disappointed by her complete disinterest with matters important to me.

Throughout the week, I spent another series of sleepless nights with wave after wave of troubling thoughts washing along the shore of my mind. Each day, further removed from the previous Saturday's session, felt heavier and darker. I knew if people could view the horrific thoughts that swam around in my mind, they'd be shocked.

By the time I arrived at Katrina's office for our next weekly appointment, my initial excitement from our last appointment had faded ... the warm-shower phenomenon again.

As I sat in Katrina's waiting area, my thoughts turned to how the daily grind of the work week had taken its toll. Things at work were starting to heat up. I was in charge of taking Thermster Technologies public. It would be the hottest Initial Public Offering (IPO) of the year and had been a major coup when our firm, Cadwallader Smythe, beat out much larger, more established investment banking firms.

My team and I had put our hearts into the sales pitch to Thermster's CEO and Board of Directors to represent them in managing their IPO. It was a career-defining opportunity. We'd been chasing Thermster for over two years, wining and dining the CEO, knowing he eventually had plans to take the company public.

Now that the time had come, the business press was all over the story, as Thermster was the latest high flyer in the area of alternative energy sources. Thermster's transformational technology can convert trash into usable energy. They've already perfected the technique of converting oil-based plastic waste into cheap energy. Thermster is also on the verge of rolling out the ability to convert other common forms of trash into a sustainable and cheap energy source. The reported rollout of this technology is fueling huge interest among prospective investors.

Thermster is a game changer in the world of alternative energy. The money raised from their IPO would be massive, putting it among the ten largest public offerings ever for technology companies, even larger than Google's IPO in 2004.

Sitting in the waiting area of Katrina's office, I found my mind wandering to the multimillion-dollar payout I'd receive for the deal. This transaction was by far the highest profile deal in the history of our firm.

So far, I'd been able to do a decent job of hiding my depression, leaning heavily on my team and pulling myself together at key moments. Though, the other, more senior, partners had been watching me closely ever since my erratic behavior started in Atlanta. I knew if I didn't somehow pull myself out of this funk, it was just a matter of time before they would consider replacing me as the lead on the deal. It was just too big, too crucial, to not have every member of the team on their A-game, particularly in my position as lead partner on the deal team.

As I aimlessly flipped through copies of *National Geographic* while waiting for Katrina, I wondered what would come next, both in today's session and in the longer term. Her methods were clearly unorthodox. *Where was all this headed?* All week, Katrina's comment suggesting that we might experience places that were "dark and far away" haunted me.

When she opened her door, she had a mischievous smile on her face. As usual, she was dressed in stylish skinny jeans. She wore a white t-shirt and a sleek black blazer with ruched sleeves, accentuated with a black necklace. I wondered what her closet at home looked like and how many articles of black clothing she owned.

Once we sat down, she got right to the point. "You have what many people aspire to … career success, good looks, physical health, and lots of money coming in … yet, you've been contemplating suicide with the same frequency that a hungry dieter thinks about food in the refrigerator. Good news is, your situation isn't unique. Every day, highly functional people just like you enter the dark and troubling world of depression, some more severe than others."

Katrina suggested that a possible explanation for my mental health challenges could be unwanted energy blockages, which she believed could be released through the type of regression therapy we explored in our last session.

She reminded me how regression therapy works. Similar to how back and shoulder pain can be relieved by releasing stored tension or negative energy, the same can be true for our mental health, she explained. Events in our distant past can negatively influence our current states of mind through energy blockages. Just being aware of the clog and understanding its root cause can lead to the release of the unwanted barrier.

"Energy blockages are a metaphysical concept, difficult to prove to a skeptical scientific community, but I assure you, Nick, they are very real."

She went on to say that our delving into my childhood memories was a good start but ultimately wouldn't solve the core issues causing my depression. "We're likely going to need to go farther back, much farther back," she said.

"Katrina, what do you mean, farther back? I was three years old when I went down the slide. There's not much farther back we can go."

"Do you remember when I asked you to suspend your current belief system and you agreed to try?" she said.

"Yes, of course I do," I replied as I tried to sit more comfortably on the couch.

With the same natural ease one orders a cup of coffee, she said, "Okay, now is the time for you to start opening your mind to the idea that this isn't your first incarnation on Earth. In fact, it's possible you've had multiple past lives."

The expression written on my face left no doubt where I stood on the matter. *Past lives? Is she serious? She was starting to sound like a nut job ... and how the hell would she know?*

Undeterred, she continued on. "Nick, the vast majority of people I've regressed have had many lives. I'm betting you're no different, particularly given the energy blockages you seem to have."

I asked if this was some kind of joke.

Fully aware that I'd likely be resistant to the idea intellectually, she said, "There's only one way to know for sure. You see, Nick, instead of regressing you to view a childhood memory, we're going to try to go back and see your soul in a past incarnation. If you're willing, all I ask is you keep an open mind to the possibility of you having past lives. If you do that, I think you'll be amazed at what you can experience."

Although I found the concept of past lives highly disagreeable, I suppose I could humor her and engage in this crazy dialogue. "How ... how is it possible to go back in time, Katrina? Even if I had past lives, it's impossible to see them ... isn't it?" I said.

"Do you remember the end of our last session? I mentioned there are three levels of consciousness: the conscious mind, the subconscious mind, and the superconscious mind."

"Yeah, of course. Although I have to admit, I've never heard the term superconscious mind before."

She explained, "Hypnosis, similar to meditation, is a technique to quiet the mind, so the relentless chatter that typically occupies the conscious mind can be silenced. It is through this silence that you become the 'observer' of your current or even your past lives. It is here that we conduct psychological forensics. Think of it as past-life archeology, which will give us a more complete understanding of who you really are ... and what is driving your current state of depression.

"Essentially, through effective relaxation and guided questioning, you're able to access higher states of consciousness. You can search deep within your subconscious mind, which contains cellular memories of your history in this life."

Katrina became more animated, using several hand gestures. She explained that the subconscious mind is like the memory storage (hard drive) on a computer, while the conscious mind is the "thinking" processor on the computer, which retrieves the data stored in the subconscious mind.

She went on to suggest that when on long drives, we occasionally day dream and later discover we've traveled a long distance but have no recollection of what occurred during the last thirty minutes. The subconscious mind successfully oversaw the driving, breathing, etc., while the conscious mind was lost in thought about other random things. We've all experienced this.

The superconscious mind, continuing with the computer analogy, is like the Internet, allowing our computer to connect into other linked computers. The superconscious mind is a star gate to knowledge and wisdom from all of our past lives. The superconscious mind existed before we were born into our current lives and will live on after our bodies die. It's our conscious minds that die, because they are tied to functioning brains.

Katrina also explained that through the superconscious mind, we can find our true identity, which some would say is our soul. The superconscious mind contains all of the accumulated wisdom gained from all of our human experiences, in both current and past lives.

She paused for a minute to let her explanation sink in and then continued. "Soul memories accessed via the superconscious mind are released into human awareness through hypnotic regression ... the kind of regression I am preparing to administer.

"When you experienced that incredible clarity of memory during your childhood review, we accessed memories coded in your subconscious mind ... while the wisdom and insights you experienced came from accessing the superconscious mind, which houses infinite wisdom, Nick."

Katrina began drawing in her notebook a diagram that showed the connections between the conscious, subconscious, and superconscious minds.

I sat up silently and carefully studied the diagram, which showed on the left of the page, a human stick figure with a conscious and subconscious mind, labeled "current life." In the middle of the page, she had labeled half a dozen stick figures "past lives." Each of the past-life stick figures also contained a conscious and subconscious mind. On the top of the page, she drew a cloud shape labeled "superconscious mind," which connected to the current-life and past-life stick figures.

These were all foreign concepts to me. *How had I never heard of the superconscious mind before? Was it the superconscious mind that had brought such clarity and wisdom during the previous week's session?* Skeptical thoughts swam throughout my head.

Seeing my overwhelmed expression, Katrina said, "Nick, we have multiple lives to advance our soul development through human learnings and experiences. We come to each life with free will. We also come to each life with a plan to experience specific karmic lessons to build upon our learnings from past lives, all with the aim of raising our vibrational energy levels.

"Through regression therapy, we may have a chance to explore karmic lessons from past lives that contain some relevance to your present life. Oftentimes, we spend several lifetimes just trying to master one or two karmic lessons to grow spiritually. This is about to get interesting, Nick."

Much of what Katrina was saying was going over my head ... vibrational energy levels, karmic lessons, accessing the superconscious ... all completely new concepts. But I was intently listening, letting it soak in without judgment. She had a comforting way about her ... a way that made me want to believe what she was saying, no matter how farfetched it seemed.

She went on to say that the secrets of life and death are concealed behind a dark veil. "We are about to look behind that veil. Are you ready, Nick?"

I was genuinely unnerved at the prospect of potentially looking behind a veil that wasn't meant to be pierced. *Is she fucking crazy?*

After a moment of uninterrupted eye contact, I shrugged my shoulders and pushed aside my anxiety with the same certainty that one has when boarding a roller coaster for the first time. *I suppose nothing really bad can happen.*

Similar to the previous week, we started with breathing and full-body exercises, feeling the golden light flow down throughout my body. In short order, I was in a total state of calm. Everything felt heavy.

Katrina continued saying in a low voice, "Now we are ready to go back farther in time, back into a past-life. Visualize a beautiful door that is closed. This is a doorway to your past lives, and on the other side of the door is a magnificent light that doesn't hurt your eyes. On the other side of the light is a scene, a person, a past-life. Join this scene as I count down from five to one. As I reach one, you will join that scene and you can remember everything.

"Five. The door begins to open and you can see the light. Four. You move through light closer and closer to the scene. Three. Coming closer. Two. Nearly there now. One. Be there now," she finished as she tapped my forehead.

She suggested that if I found myself in a body, I should look down and observe what type of clothes I had on and to pay special attention to any people, surrounding objects, colors, and geography.

I began talking lightly and deliberately again. The year 1820 popped into my mind's eye. When I looked down, I saw the body of a tall, muscular black man wearing loose-fitting overalls and beat-up brown shoes caked with brownish-red dirt and clay.

I began to see crisp and clear images of a time long past. It was like seeing a high-definition TV a few feet in front of me, similar in clarity to the childhood memory I encountered from the previous week. *It appears I'm a slave, likely in the American Deep South.*

She asked, "Do you see other people? Does anyone seem familiar?"

I responded that I saw a slave woman. *She is a large, thick-boned woman, perhaps one hundred sixty pounds, and black-skinned like me. It's obvious we are in love. I'm seeing two names pop into my field of vision. The name given by our slave owners is Sarah, but her private name is Comba, which is the name we use in the slave quarters. We use private names in defiance to show each other the white people can't take all of our identity. My names are Joe and Taynay.*

Comba is pregnant. We are having our first baby together. It's a rare spring afternoon that we're not working in the fields. She is wearing a heavily worn, dusted pink dress that is fraying at the ankles from heavy usage. It's her only piece of clothing that isn't designed for working. Comba looks absolutely beautiful in her own way. Not a classic beauty, but a smile that is so appealing and authentic that it takes my breath away. We live together in slave quarters, essentially a small one room wooden shack on the plantation. It has one door and no windows, and the rotting wood roof leaks terribly when it rains.

It's clear we have a hard life, but there is tremendous love between us. Comba and I have been the best of friends since childhood. We were both born on the plantation. We seem to accept our lot in life, so long as we have each other to share our lives with and depend upon. We're very happy together despite our conditions.

Up to this point, we've spent nearly this entire life's journey together. Life as a slave can be incredibly lonely, filled with emptiness, hopelessness, and dark despair. Comba and I bring light to each other's darkness. In explaining our love for each other, I can hear her telling me that all the immense darkness in the entire world still can't put out the light from a single star.

Now I'm going back and viewing the first time I noticed her as a child. Her smile catches my attention with a single glance, even as a young five-year-old child. My father and I are sitting on a wooden bench at dusk, eating peaches as she walks over. She's about three years old and asks if she can have a peach. She's hungry and hasn't eaten all day. I look at my father for approval and hand her our last one.

I'm now seeing images of her bringing countless smiles to my face over the years. We touched each other's hearts on so many levels. As adults, on this particular hot summer *night, we are laying outside and talking for hours. We're staring up at the stars without a care in the world. It's cooler outside than in our overheated living quarters. I can see her nestling the back of her head on the precise spot where my right arm connects to my shoulder. She is saying it's her special nook and claims it as her spot for all time. My slave face is awash in proud smiles and my soul is flooded with love for her.*

Evenings are our only moments of peace, as we are field slaves, which entails working outside from sunrise to sunset on most days. It's clear we live in constant fear of being separated from each other and from our son. Our owner is old and sick. When he dies, the possibility of separation is very real, as some of us will be indiscriminately sold off or distributed to his relatives. Over the years, many of the slave children have been taken from their parents and sold to neighboring plantations.

Katrina asked me to go to a significant moment in this slave life and describe what is happening to me.

Its years later now. I see Comba lying in our sleeping area inside the shack, which is essentially a thick, miserable blanket on the floor. She is very weak and frail. She has lost at least forty pounds and is clearly dying. Her face has been transformed into a skeletal shadow of her once-full face. Her previously pudgy cheeks are completely sunken in.

I'm slowly stroking her hair, much of which is gone. Her brown skin is badly wrinkled and dry. Only her eyes, her bright brown eyes, show signs of life. Comba has a disease of some kind, but we don't know what it is. There are no doctors to help her. She's in her late twenties, similar age as me.

Still in the highly relaxed state lying on Katrina's couch, I could feel a lump in my throat forming. I had tears in my eyes and felt a wave of intense sadness sweep through my body, as if I were really on the plantation. The emotions felt absolutely real. Of course, I was conscious that I was not really there with Comba, but it felt so real. *Damn, I love her ... with all my heart,* I realized.

Katrina, sensing my sadness asked, "Nick, are you okay to move to the next significant event in this life?"

I manage a weak nod and continue, *I'm pleading with my overseers and owners to get Comba medical attention, but they won't. I'm desperate and begin fighting with them. They are holding me down, and I'm being beaten mercilessly.*

There are four of them. They are kicking me in the midsection and face with their heavy, black, dusty boots. One of them picks up an oblong-shaped stone the size of a softball and throws it at me with deadly intentions. It hits my ribcage squarely and cracks several ribs. They continue kicking and punching me while laughing and yelling obscenities at me. My back and ribcage are in excruciating pain as blood pours down my face from a broken nose and a large gash just above my left eye.

Following a short pause, images appeared of Comba as she approached her moment of death, openly suffering. I saw that as her husband, I was devastated and despondent.

At the same time, as Nick, I experienced a strong intuition that there's something familiar about Comba. I couldn't place her in my life as Nick, but the smile she flashed, even on her deathbed, seemed incredibly familiar, as if I'd seen it before and had been mesmerized by it.

Katrina said, "Okay, try to sit in front of her and look directly through her eyes into her head. You are looking into her soul. See if you recognize her. You may see a face appear behind her eyes that you are familiar with in this lifetime."

Sitting next to Comba, I put my hands on each side of her face and tried to look through her bright brown eyes. She wore a wanting, aching look as she gazed directly into my eyes. It was as if she wanted me to recognize her. I could see a female face forming from a misty, vapor-like smoke appearing inside her head. The facial features had a unique familiarity, but the face was not formed enough for me to make out exactly who it belonged to.

Now, I'm seeing visions of me holding Comba's limp right hand, fingers intertwined together. Faintly, she is mouthing words to me, so weak that her voice is barely audible.

"Taynay, look into my eyes. Please don't let go of my hand till I'm gone. I want to touch you ... I want to touch the hands of love when I pass to the other side."

In a matter of moments, her eyes close and she is gone.

After we reviewed several other scenes from that life, Katrina asked me to fast-forward to my body's death in that lifetime.

Images began to appear of me in the slave body at a much older age. *I'm a white-haired old man lying on my stomach. My face is leaning over a makeshift cot. I can see the floor of my shack, the same shack Comba and I lived in together. I notice details I'd never noticed before, such as small splinters; the knots in the old, worn-out, rotting wood; and the flat heads of the nails holding the floorboards in. The splinters on the floorboards are the last sight I see before I close my eyes as Taynay one last time.*

The shack is full of people gathered around my lifeless body. Comba and I have one child, who is now in his thirties. *We have several grandchildren, as well. The other slaves are crying. It is clear there is tremendous love in the room.*

Katrina asked me to exit Taynay's body and float above the scene. "What do you think are the key lessons from your life as Taynay?"

Answers again began to stream into my mind from a source of greater intelligence ... the same source I had experienced in the childhood memory ... the superconscious mind, presumably.

Occasionally, a soul will select a life filled with hardship, tragedy, or difficulties in order to quicken its spiritual learning. This life is not retribution for past misdeeds, nor the manifestation of bad karma. To round out our learning, we come back as different genders, levels of affluence, and ethnicities in order to experience the many angles of life. Souls don't possess such demographic characteristics.

A knowing began to sink in that a life experiencing real hardships and challenging relationships offers the potential for accelerated soul growth. *My life as Taynay contained terribly difficult obstacles. I was born into a life of slavery, forced to live in squalor. Life on the plantation was grueling, where work was never-ending. There were white men on horses who had long bullwhips and oversaw us in the fields each day.*

Although the slave owners had a claim on my body, they didn't have a claim on my thoughts or my soul. In my life as Taynay, I never fully realized this concept. After Comba died, her memory was with me every remaining day. Images of her smiling face consumed me like an overhead light consumes a room's darkness.

But, thoughts of hatred co-existed in me. I spent the rest of my life mired in bitterness toward my owners. I let their tyranny and domination of my physical body break my spirit. I died a broken, dispirited, depressed old man who sadly would never love again.

Katrina whispered, "How do you think the lessons of this slave lifetime connect to your current life? Are there understandings that will help you remove any blockages to inner peace and joy and happiness in this life?"

The insights continued to stream in all at once. *The knowing that souls often choose difficult lives turned my sense of perspective completely upside down. For example, a child born with a genetic deficiency isn't someone to be pitied; rather, he is a soul that's here to teach us something about compassion and unconditional love for those less fortunate. In my current life, I've tended to judge and stereotype people who are less fortunate, less wealthy, or less attractive than me. As Nick, I have regularly judged people, assessing their stations in life. There is no joy or inner peace that comes from comparing my situation in life to someone else's situation. I understand that now.*

A second key knowing involves the concept of "attachment and detachment." The early years of my life as Taynay were comprised of moments of hopeless despair offset by affectionate love when I was with Comba and my son. The reason Comba and I were happy together is we were able to periodically "detach" from the horrific conditions of being slaves and "attach" to making a life together, comprised of unconditional love for each other. She taught me how to be happy. This represented tremendous spiritual progress for both of our souls ... by learning to not let our level of happiness be determined by outside circumstances.

We were each born into our lives alone. We had an amazing journey together as lovers, parents, and best friends in life. Our journeys ended at different points, but for those twenty-five years that our paths overlapped, it was a glorious set of experiences, where we each experienced a form of oneness.

Following Comba's death, I struggled with detaching from my terrible conditions more than ever before. My mind became a prisoner to memories of past injustices. Comba fully understood that when you are consciously detached from the circumstances that surround you, it opens you up to enjoying all of the good cheer and wonderment that life has to offer. She learned to let negativity flow right through her with minimal impact on her degree of happiness.

Comba understood these lessons when her body died. I never really did. I missed an opportunity to let go or detach from the bitterness and hatred that plagued the rest of my life as Taynay. I could have chosen to dedicate the rest of my life to the memory of Comba by attaching to being a better father and by spreading light and warmth to all those that I loved. This was a missed opportunity for me to raise my vibrational level and grow spiritually.

In my life as Nick, some of the same issues that plagued Taynay are present, although my life as Taynay was a much more difficult one. Oftentimes as Nick, I've had a habit of attaching my daily mood to the trivial mini-successes and mini-disappointments of the day. It's a dysfunction that plagues the vast majority of people, although it is particularly pronounced in me. Trivial, largely irrelevant outcomes such as whether my seats at the Bears game are good, or whether the dry cleaner removed the stain on my shirt, or whether I had to wait long for seating to open up at the restaurant, or whether my annual raise was big enough. These all falsely impact my level of happiness.

Katrina brought me back to a waking state of consciousness, and she and I discussed the regression in great detail. We spent much of our time focused on how knowings from past lives can release energy blockages and can cause psychological healing. Despite seeing the wretched slave life that Taynay had endured, I was no longer leery of piercing the veil.

As I was walking out, Katrina asked me to ponder a question for our next session. "Do you believe your true authentic self is housed in your physical body, or do you believe it is housed in something non-physical, such as a soul?"

Suffering from Attachment

After the session with Katrina in which I saw my life as Taynay, I worked almost non-stop on the Thermster deal. I found that if I kept my mind occupied by work, The Darkness would slip back into its cave temporarily.

The next Saturday, once I was in Katrina's office and after the usual chitchat, Katrina's tone turned more direct. "Okay, Nick, you've had a week to ponder what we experienced in the regression."

I'd given the regression careful thought and concluded that if it's true that we have multiple lives, I'd have to reexamine my entire philosophy on life. Katrina seemed to be suggesting a move away from my current perspective of believing I'm a body that is born once and dies once ... and a move toward believing I'm a soul that simply changes form and comes back over and over again. It was a lot to digest ... and a fundamental shift in perspective on the mysteries of life and death.

"Honestly, I'm not sure what to believe," I said. "Maybe it was just a hallucination or dream fantasy created by my mind? Do you think I am just making this up while I'm in a trance? It seems so bizarre, being a slave in Alabama."

She explained that past-life regression is controversial, with zealots on both sides of the argument, but there are facts not in dispute.

"The scientific data is absolutely overwhelming that some past-life memories are based on verifiable real people and real events, that the person under hypnosis would have no way of knowing. I personally have reviewed many documented cases by legitimate, impartial researchers that prove this point to any fair-minded skeptic," she explained.

"There are other points that suggest the validity of past-life memories. For example, how do we explain a woman under hypnosis suddenly speaking Mandarin Chinese fluently with a dialect from 600 years ago … when in her current life, she's never spoken a word of Mandarin Chinese? How do we explain when two people independently go under hypnosis and recall the same obscure details of the exact same past-life event … except the past-life memory is seen from the two differing viewpoints of their respective past-life bodies? I could go on and on.

"Nick, in my view, the real question isn't whether past-life memories are possible. I think that has been soundly answered by the scientific data. The real question is, when are we seeing real past-life memories and when are we just seeing a metaphor or hallucination created by our subconscious mind?"

She went on to say that this is a difficult question to answer. Most past-life memories are not easily verifiable, so we use a handful of indicators that help us assess whether the memories being recalled are likely real or fantasy. For example, a positive indicator is the subject experiencing intense emotions during the regression. Of course, that's not scientific proof but certainly is a positive indicator of the realness of the memory.

Katrina explained that she also looks for general historical accuracy. For example, if the subject is viewing a scene in which there are obvious historical inaccuracies, such as someone being shot by a rifle in a time before rifles had been invented, there is reason to suspect it is more likely a metaphor or fantasy. There are a handful of other positive and negative indicators as well.

"That's very helpful," I said. "Do you think what I saw … the slave life … was real or fantasy?"

"It's difficult to be absolutely certain, but based on the vividness of the details, emotional intensity, general historical accuracy, I'd say it's likely the slave life you experienced was a past-life. Why would you create a fantasy of being a slave in the Deep South living a life of squalor? Especially since you've haven't had any meaningful interaction or connection to that era or period of injustice. Make sense, Nick?"

"I think so," I replied. "But I have to be honest. Despite what you just said, my skeptical mind is still saying this is absolutely crazy."

She nodded and smiled. "Is it crazy that when I blow a dog whistle, you hear nothing, yet a dog can hear it clearly? Is it crazy that a bee can detect ultraviolet light to help it find nectar, but you cannot? Is it crazy that we can't sense radio or television waves, yet we know they are always there? You and I are limited to experiencing the world through the prism of our five senses, Nick. Isn't it possible there are other vibrational frequencies, energies, or phenomena that we can't sense? Isn't it possible that we experience only a narrow sliver of reality?"

Sensing that I was trying to understand her reasoning, she added, "All I ever ask is you continue to keep an open mind and decide for yourself. As we saw last week, one can make a case that our bodies and conscious minds die but our souls are eternal and can come back over and over again. Identifying with your authentic self, your soul rather than your body, is a fundamentally different lens from which to view your life. It could lead you to a new depth of self-understanding."

I said, "I'm still confused. I realize I've consciously designed my life around achievement and wealth creation. But hey, these are laudable and worthy pursuits … just as much as spiritual growth is. Are you saying my life pursuits up to this point have been misguided and all wrong?"

She paused for a moment, seemingly pondering whether two contradictory positions could both be true. "That's an interesting question. Let's do another regression today. I'm going to adjust our hypnosis process slightly, to target one of your past lives most relevant to the question. If we get lucky, we may find some answers, although I can't promise we will. Whatever we see today, please remember, the past-life hypnosis we are experiencing may point to the idea that you have an immortal soul who continually learns and develops by living many physical lives."

I got comfortably flat on the couch to signal my readiness, and we began the relaxation process. Once I'd reached a total state of calm throughout my body and mind, we went through the usual process to access my past memories.

Katrina guided me as she had the previous week. "On the other side of the door is a light. It's the type of light that doesn't hurt your eyes, and just beyond it is a scene, a person, a past-life. It's a life of yours that could involve questions of achievement and material wealth creation. If there is such a life of yours, join it as I count down from five to one ..."

As she tapped my forehead, the "1900's" appeared in my mind's eye almost immediately, and I began to speak. *My senses tell me I'm in Europe, likely an Italian coastal city in the early 1900's. I'm a short male, perhaps 5'6", and rather plump, in my mid-thirties. I'm walking around giving instructions to the supervisors of the dock workers, who are generally large, brawny men.*

There's an annoying smell emanating from the nearby fishing boats that hovers in one's senses. Only a brisk wind can give temporary relief from the awful stench, although I'm obviously used to it, having been on the docks much of my adult life.

The docks are a bustling scene with a frenzy of activity. It appears I'm a successful shipping merchant, likely upper middle class for the time period.

Katrina asked me to go to a significant event in this life.

After a brief period of seeing nothing, I began to see images appearing. *I'm younger, perhaps early twenties. It's my wedding day. I'm very excited and nervous, very fidgety. There's a group of a hundred or so people gathered at the church. My bride is wearing a veil, so I can't see her face.*

She's wearing a long, flowing, patterned dress that covers her slim body from neck to toe. She has long, dark brown curly hair pulled up on the top of her head. Her hair is laced in an intricate pattern of pink ribbons and curly weaves.

I'm lifting her veil now. My eyes are captivated by her every feature ... large Maria Bartiroma eyes; a small, perfectly formed nose; and soft pink lips. She is strikingly beautiful and has a smile on her lips. My bride is much more attractive than I am. We're both happy and clearly excited to be marrying. We're in love.

Katrina asked if the woman looked familiar to me.

Physically, I've never seen her before in this life as Nick, but when she looks away for a split second and then looks back at me smiling, her mannerisms and facial expressions are eerily similar, almost identical, to Comba's. Attracting me like a high-powered magnet, she tilts her head at the exact same angle, splits her lips and adjusts her jaw just as Comba did when she smiled. Her name is Allesandra in this incarnation, but it's clearly the same soul as Comba's that I am marrying. The name Peitro is coming into my vision, which must be my name in this life.

"Nick, similar to what we tried in your slave life, put your hands on her face and look through her eyes. See if you can make out a face familiar in your life as Nick."

Soul Sessions

My hands are on the sides of Allesandra's face now. As I'm looking through her eyes I can see the white vapor-like smoke forming into Comba's facial features.

Katrina asked me to keep looking, stay with it, and see if the vapor morphs into another face.

I can see another face forming that looks familiar, but again, I can't seem to recognize exactly who it is. Definitely not a family member, and it's not Janice or Kelly.

The white mist slowly faded away, and we moved to the next significant event in Peitro's life.

I'm with Allesandra. We've been married for fifteen years or so and have several children together. We're arguing. She's upset that I'm always working at the docks. The hours are brutally long.

She's more disappointed than angry. We hardly spend quality time together anymore. It's clear I'm trying the best I can to provide a secure living for our family. I run a midsize shipping business. I'm seeing images of me striving and clawing to build up the business. Money has been very tight at times. My major focus in life has been trying to gather wealth and local prestige, and expand my mini shipping empire. It's obvious the image I try to project to others is highly important to me, perhaps more than the depth of my character that remains hidden beneath.

Suffering from Attachment

"Why is this argument significant?" Katrina asked.

It's not clear to me why the argument has relevance.

After a moment, I continue. *It's later that morning now. Allesandra and I are at our dinner table. We're smiling and quietly listening to our two youngest children, Samuele and Lena, talking and playing with each other on the wood floor next to the eating area. Our kids are everything to us. Much of our joy in life comes from the time we spend together watching them, nurturing them, and loving them. It's an eternal bond that has deepened our love for each other.*

I'm continuing to apologize to her that I haven't been helping out at home as much as I should have. But at the same time, I'm rationalizing my behavior, commenting about how far we've come financially. We've finally got a little breathing room.

Even though we've been together for many years, I often feel the urge to try to impress her with accomplishments and status. I'm telling her there is an upcoming exclusive local dinner party we've been invited to. I know I'm not physically attractive, and deep down, it's my misguided way to try to keep a hold on her. I've always been insecure about my looks.

She knows my frailties and complexes better than anyone, including myself. She simply doesn't care about the dinner party. It's written all over her face: she just wants to spend more time with me. My slavish work hours have been a low-simmering, ongoing dispute between us for several years.

"What else are you seeing, Nick?" Katrina asked.

Since childhood, Allesandra has struggled with her own self-esteem issues. I'm seeing images of me holding her tightly … the side of her head nestled in the curve of my shoulder as she cries hysterically, the same curve that Comba declared as hers for all time. Despite Allesandra's physical beauty, she has spent long periods of her life not liking herself. Other than our children, I've been the one person in her life who uplifts her and helps her temporarily break the cycle of sadness.

Allesandra is telling me I'm the only person that's been able to understand her … the one man who can see past the many masks she creates for others … the one man among hundreds she's crossed paths with who she instantly felt safe with, safe enough to spend a lifetime together. Her words are hovering in my memory and carry the sweet color of unconditional love.

I'm seeing scenes of us taking long walks along the sandy dirt path that runs along the cliffs overlooking the Mediterranean Sea. Few words are said, as there is no need. We're completely absorbed in the moment, right now together, as if we were the only two people in the world. When my hand reaches out and finds hers, at that moment, it's as if we're able to touch each other's pure essence ... which houses our most hidden fears and most precious hopes.

With the sea in the background, my eyes are met by her smile and shy laugh. I'm often left with feelings of wonderment ... wonderment at how a strikingly beautiful woman like Allesandra can thirst for love from someone as ordinary as me.

Short vignettes continue to come through ... how my habit of sliding Allesandra's long brown hair behind her left ear is always met with a loving smile ... how her arm fits perfectly underneath and around mine as we stroll arm in arm ... how her skirt gathers around her legs and sand particles cling under her feet just a few dozen steps after her shoes come off ... how a simple parting of her lips leaves me feeling like I'm the luckiest man alive.

In the next scene revealed to me, I'm down at the docks talking with a group of my supervisors. A gust of wind blows some scrolled papers out of my hands. Without realizing the impending importance of the moment, we're chasing the windblown, scattered scrolls around the dock area. I'm crouching down to pick up one of the papers and I get too close to the back of an unattended, tied up horse.

With one swift and powerful "back-kick" to the side of my skull, he strikes a deathblow.

As Nick, I'm forcing myself to watch the images, as a silent scream begins to build up inside me. It's as if an invisible thief has just stolen Pietro's life away.

I can see onlookers viewing my lifeless body lying face up, eyes open but lifeless, rolled up toward the top of my head. One of my supervisors is frantically trying to revive me by shouting and shaking me. There is a noticeable indentation on my head that matches the shape of the iron horseshoe that struck me. Oddly, there is very little blood on the scene. Just a small trickle slowly seeping from the cut above my left eye.

As Nick, I don't feel physical pain watching my life as Peitro end. However, there is a real sense of emotion ... the silent scream has morphed into sadness as Peitro swallowed the bitter pill of not saying good-bye to Allesandra or his children. Sadness that he's leaving this life with so many things still to do. Sadness that he won't see his children grow up. Peitro's life ended suddenly and unexpectedly, as many lives did back then. Only then did I realize what a wretched feeling it is to not say goodbye.

"Nick, let's have you exit Peitro's body and float above the scene. What do you see next?"

Suffering from Attachment

Before I could reply, Katrina asked, "Why do you think this life was selected for you to view? Are there key lessons from your life as Peitro that are relevant to your life as Nick?"

Similar to before, answers began to stream into my mind from a source of greater intelligence. *A key spiritual learning from Peitro's life is "most forms of suffering come from attachment" ... attachment to possessions ... attachment to results ... attachment to unfulfilled desires ... attachment to other people's opinions. Detachment is one of the most important spiritual lessons to learn. Breaking attachments can lead to authentic freedom.*

For several lifetimes, I've struggled to grasp this concept. In my life as Taynay, I was attached to my anger and hatred toward my slave owners. It was resistance that caused my suffering in that lifetime. When we accept realities that are unalterable in our lives, such as Comba being dead and me being a slave, then and only then can we break free of the negative thought patterns and enjoy the positive aspects of life.

These were not random thoughts stumbling into my mind, I realized; rather, they were being fed to me like medicine in an IV drip. Surprised, but somewhat detached from this realization, I continued to speak.

Don't be in conflict with "what is." Make positive change when we can, but have the wisdom to detach from circumstances that simply cannot be changed. By understanding conscious detachment, we free ourselves from obsessive preoccupation with needing to accumulate wealth ... needing other people to like us ... or needing to feel important, which are all negative vibrational frequencies born from the ego.

More insights continued to flow in, and I continued to repeat them aloud. *Detaching from negative thought patterns is the polar opposite of repressing feelings. Detachment occurs when we look at circumstances and acknowledge their presence, but we understand they do not define us. Understanding this is a fundamental breakthrough.*

When we engage in repressing feelings, the attachment remains, which causes the suffering to continue ... whether it be Peitro suffering from "not having enough" or Taynay suffering from unalterable circumstances.

From a relationship perspective, detachment doesn't involve weakening or deserting a positive, loving relationship, but it does mean discontinuing unhealthy dependency on other people, particularly intimate relationships. True love for another person is never predicated on attachment. In my life as Peitro, my insecurities and dependency on Allesandra's love led me down an egoic path of trying to hold on to her through wealth accumulation.

For two consecutive lives, a key karmic lesson for my soul to learn was that most forms of suffering come from attachment.

As Katrina brought me back to a waking state of consciousness, I wondered if the linkage between suffering and attachment was the fundamental breakthrough I'd been seeking.

While an entirely new set of questions swirled around in my head, what really fascinated me was the notion of Comba appearing as Allesandra.

As if this past-life stuff weren't already crazy enough, my reincarnating with the same soul in two separate lives as husband and wife was mind-blowing. It couldn't be a coincidence, as the probabilities are astronomical. Of course, I'd heard of the concept of soul mates but never had studied it. *Is this what I was experiencing ... a sudden and mysterious revelation?*

"Well Nick," Katrina asked, "what are your thoughts on your life as Peitro?"

"I have to admit, this is getting crazier by the minute. I don't even know where to start," I said.

"What's so crazy?" she asked.

I glanced at the clock, somewhat dejected by seeing the time. "I know we're out of time again, but I'd really like to talk more about Comba and Allesandra being the same soul. I'm wondering if there is such a thing as a soul mate. Is her soul somewhere on Earth today? If so, where? Is she eventually going to come into my life?"

For the first time in as long as I can remember, I wondered if there was someone out there waiting for me.

Soul Mates

Throughout the week, our team worked hard to understand the guts of Thermster's technology. We needed Thermster's help to properly represent the company's capabilities for our investment pitches. We weren't making much progress. Their senior management seemed to gloss over our questions or to want to just plain stonewall.

As I awoke on Saturday, I decided to leave early for my appointment with Katrina so I could stop by a local diner and have a peaceful breakfast. It was a welcome few moments of peace. I turned off my phone and reflected on the insights from my lives as Taynay and Peitro. After some careful reflection and an amazing pancake breakfast, I walked into Katrina's lobby with more questions than answers.

I turned on my iPhone, as relentlessly checking messages is an obsession I know I'll never break. I hadn't heard from Janice in two days. She was in Florida, staying at the swanky Delano Hotel on Miami Beach with a group of her girlfriends. I assumed she was up to no good, since she hadn't returned the couple of texts I'd sent her asking how the trip was going. Her Facebook page was populated with a ridiculous number of sexy bikini poses and drunk party pics with people I didn't recognize.

Once the phone had turned on, an unusual number of vibrations and beeps sounded, indicating multiple new messages. Several texts from Ridge Christensen, a senior manager working for me on the Thermster deal, caught my eye. Ridge was putting together materials for our upcoming road show to large institutional investors.

"Call me ASAP" *8:38 am*

"Left you a VM. Call me. It's URGENT" *8:45 am*

"Where are you? Pls call" 8:55 *am*

As I was reading the texts, Katrina emerged from behind her door. "Nick, great to see you. Let's get started," she said as she turned, expectantly waiting for me to follow.

Ridge's crisis probably wasn't a crisis. I'd call him after my session. I sent him a quick text saying, "Call you at 1 pm," and turned off my phone. He could wait.

Despite challenges on the Thermster deal all week, all I could think was ... *Why is the same woman appearing in both past lives I've seen so far? Who is she? Is it possible to have a soul mate? What exactly is a soul mate?* I had struggled to concentrate at work and could barely sleep all week.

"Katrina, I was so tempted to call you to see if we could schedule time earlier in the week. I'm a mess at work. I can't stop thinking about past lives and the feeling of unconditional love I experienced for Comba and Allesandra. If you don't mind, I'd like to spend the first half of our session today talking about the concept of soul mates. I can't get it out of my head. I'm seduced by the concept."

"Sure, let's do it. By the way, if we need it, I've set aside additional time for us today," she said enthusiastically.

"Great. I have a lot of questions, Katrina, but it's probably better if you just start talking about the concept of soul mates, and I'll ask clarifying questions."

She said, "We have soul mates, multiple soul mates. As far as we can tell, nearly everyone has a soul group. Research on reincarnation suggests five to twenty members."

She continued schooling me, teaching me that soul mates are eternal partners who come into our lives and remind us of our life plans. They often help us step out from behind the masks we've built for everyone else and challenge us to grow spiritually. When in a soul mate's presence, we often sense authentic love for who we really are, not our pretend masks.

Sometimes we are paired as spouses, but not always. Soul mates can come in many forms. Sometimes we are siblings, friends, lovers, parent and child, or in other close relationships.

Soul mates radiate similar vibrational frequencies. Once two soul mates brush up against each other, they tend to have a sense of curiosity about each other and an inexplicable strong attraction. Often their age difference can be substantial, which creates further confusion.

At first, the allure may be sexual in nature, due to the intensity of the early encounters. However, our souls are not attracted to conventional social structures such as dating or marriage. Rather, soul mates are partnered to further spiritual learnings and each other's growth.

The amount of time that soul mates are in our lives varies and could involve a single encounter or a lifelong journey together. No doubt you've heard the saying that people come into our lives for a reason, a season, or a lifetime. This is very true for soul mates. It's not uncommon for a person to have a soul mate linger in his or her memory for years and wonder what might have been, even if the initial brush was brief.

I was mesmerized listening to Katrina, hanging on every word. Deep truths seemed to tumble off her lips like products off an assembly line. I wanted to get a pad and paper to start taking notes. Everything she was saying rang true to me and helped explain what I'd felt for Comba and Allesandra in my memories. Throughout the past two weeks, I'd experienced an intense love lurking just beneath the surface of my awareness. It was different, the depth and breadth of which was more than anything I'd ever felt before ... like a vast, underground spring.

Katrina's lecture continued while I did my best to absorb her words. Soul mates immediately connect on a deeper level than people in our other relationships, she explained, and as it grows, the relationship with a soul mate feels symbiotic. Soul mates get to the point where they challenge each other and, often times, confront their human frailties head-on ... together. Conversations between soul mates are unusually authentic, where deep truths and conflicts can be explored without judgment ... without masks.

When someone comes across a soul mate, it is important to resist possessive behavior ... which is a negative frequency, not healthy for the soul. This is a complex and very hard truth for us to accept as humans. Moving beyond the need to possess allows the person to move from "human-based" conditional love to "soul-based" unconditional love.

There is a knowing, a yearning, a sense of peace and charm when one is in a soul mate's presence that is different from the feeling in other relationships. Time with soul mates often feels light and breezy and yet very confusing, Katrina explained. It can feel nearly impossible to get soul mates out of our thoughts. We think about them all the time, and random daily experiences are continual reminders of their presence.

She continued, "If you can look at yourself with love and you are open to having someone come into your life, then your soul mate might arrive at just the right time, when you least expect it. Soul mates often appear from the most unlikely of circumstances."

Soul mate encounters can lead to heartache ... sometimes. For many people, meeting a soul mate is the first time they've felt maximum vulnerability, which involves a loss of control over their heart. Often, this is too much too fast and one party decides to run. The "runner" struggles to move on for much of the rest of his or her life. Sure, the runner eventually finds someone else to love, but it's not the same ... and the person often lives a life marked with a tinge of regret, wondering "what might have been." It's fear that causes the runner phenomenon, which can lead to indescribable anguish for both.

Many questions came to mind as Katrina had become animated again. I had to interrupt her to say, "What makes no sense to me is how soul mates are reunited. There are so many people we come across in a lifetime, so many choices that lead to divergent paths. What if I'd been sold to a different plantation owner in my life as Taynay? I'd never have come into contact with Comba. It's almost statistically impossible to cross paths with a soul mate unless you are born as family members, such as father and daughter. See what I mean?"

"Nick, organizing an incarnation is an incredibly complex undertaking," she said matter-of-factly, as if it were the most normal thing she'd ever uttered.

Unable to shove aside my skepticism, I said, "You're kidding right? Organizing? C'mon. You don't expect me to believe our lives are planned out in advance. If they were, then what would be the point of living the life? It's madness," I said, expecting her to be a little flustered.

Instead, she sat up in her chair and leaned forward. "Well, there's evidence that points to the notion that there's a blueprint created by your soul before you are born into each life. The blueprint includes what your karmic learning opportunities could involve. Think of it as a synopsis of how your life could play out, but please know, the future isn't a series of preordained events. Your blueprint may or may not come to fruition. Events are not etched in stone. They are completely variable and can be altered by free choice."

She went on. "Typically, a soul mate is part of the blueprint and is intended to be part of your life. Sometimes things go awry and the soul mates don't reunite in that lifetime … and sometimes they do."

I had a hard time believing that we choose our experiences and design a plan for our lives before we are re-incarnated. Intellectually, wrapping my mind around such a complex undertaking was proving difficult.

Katrina and I challenged each other's thinking on this topic. I found it intriguing to discuss something of substance like this rather than Janice's idiotic lineup of reality shows.

"My experience with conducting hundreds of regressions shows every one of us has a life plan, yet we also have free will. Basically, we map out 'destiny points' that, if all goes according to plan, will occur. What you do with the destiny points is affected by your free will and is entirely up to you. I realize this may be counterintuitive, but destiny points and free will coexist in harmony."

She paused for a moment, seemingly debating what to say next. "Nick, if you don't believe me, it's possible for you to see your life blueprint ... for your current life as Nick."

"Whaaaat? You have to be fucking joking," I stammered, trying to fight off disbelief. Once again, I couldn't get comfortable on that damn couch, which I suddenly realized sits unusually low to the ground.

She sensed my curiosity and general discomfort with the topic. "Nick, it's called a 'between-lives' regression, and here's how it works. Following the physical death of a human body, the soul exits the body and returns to the spirit world. The return is often described by those who've had a near death experience or past-life regression as being pulled, similar to a strong gravitational pull into a tunnel toward a bright light.

"Once the soul reenters the spirit world, it's often greeted by other members of its soul group or a sprit guide ... more on spirit guides later, Nick. The spirit world is essentially a space for the soul to transition into a higher form of vibrational energy and reflect on its most recent life. The soul also begins the process of making plans for its next incarnation. These plans include choice of a specific body, soul group members it will reincarnate with, and the karmic lessons the soul wants to explore, which essentially comprise the *meaning of that life*."

I sat, blown away, as Katrina went on to explain that each soul has a unique immortal character, which is joined with the human body and brain to form a human ego that produces the personality for that lifetime. Other soul group members go through the same process in concert with each other, all under the direction of more spiritually advanced spirit guides.

"Between-lives regression can help us answer the most fundamental questions such as Who am I? Why am I here? What is my purpose in this life? What have I accomplished so far? Where have I fallen short? What is my soul purpose from this point forward?" Katrina said.

"We can likely access the superconscious mind to reveal what happened in your most recent period in the spirit world just before you were born into your life as Nick," she went on. "I can't predict what you will encounter or what you will experience. This is a veil that not everyone is psychologically ready to pierce, but I'm willing to help you if you want to take a look, Nick."

This is fucking crazy, was all I could think. *Sheer and utter madness. But what if she's right? What if we have access to the most fundamental and perplexing questions in life? What if?*

Between Lives

Still wondering *what if*, I assumed my usual position of lying comfortably on Katrina's long couch, covered with the royal blue blanket. I wondered if my life would ever be the same again when I woke up in two hours.

After completing the usual relaxation techniques, I reached a highly relaxed state of six to eight brain waves per second.

Katrina asked me to search for the most recent incarnation prior to my life as Nick. She told me we would not be focusing on this most recent life, but rather, would use it as a gateway to finding my most recent between-lives period.

Similar to before, she tapped my forehead and asked me to "be there."

After a long period of blank space, images began to trickle into my mind's eye, images of a young Asian man, and I began to speak. *I'm a soldier, fighting in a war. It appears to be Vietnam, and I'm in the Viet Cong army. I split my time between being a soldier and a rural farmer. My name is Binh, and I'm in my mid-twenties.*

Katrina asked me to go directly to my death scene in that life. Instead, images of my wife and daughter traveling alone into the city to buy supplies fill my head. Images appeared rapidly and then disappeared just as quickly. My vision was transported to a scene of me with other family members ... my father and brother. I sensed that my mother died when I was a child. I explained all of this to Katrina and kept explaining the visions as they appeared.

Visions of underground tunnels are beginning to appear. It's clear I spend a lot of my time in tunnels, transporting supplies for the war effort. Life in the tunnels is awful, as we have limited food, water, and fresh air. The tunnels are rampant with poisonous snakes and creepy insects.

When I'm not seeing visions of living in tunnels, I see visions of myself living with my wife, daughter, father, and brother in a modest-sized hut-like structure. The hut has a dense, brown thatched palm leaf roof and is in what appears to be a small farming village. Our hut contains a dried mud bunker that we hide in if there is any bombing in the area, essentially acting as a primitive air-raid shelter.

Our village is in what the Americans call a free-fire zone, which means everyone in our village can be considered the enemy. Our village had one previous search-and-destroy mission conducted against it years ago by the American military. Many in our village are active Viet Cong.

I'm seeing chaos in the village. Huge explosions are all around us. It's all over very quickly. Napalm bombs dropped from an American plane land close to our hut and release a deadly ocean of fire, killing me almost instantly, as well as my brother and father. I could feel the overwhelming wave of heat flow throughout my body as I lay on Katrina's couch.

"Nick, we're not going to focus on Binh's life today, so I'd like you to exit his body and float above the scene. Are you able to do that?" Katrina whispered.

I was able to do that, and I described it as I did. *All that is left of my body are some unrecognizable charred remains. I'm exiting through the top of my head. I'm in the form of an energy mass that is steam-like in its composition. I look like I'm a puff of dense white vapor that just came out of a fog machine, but the fog is brightly lit and defined in its shape. I'm suspended, floating above the scene. I'm weightless, but I can control my movements easily. I'm still tethered to Binh's badly charred body, although faintly.*

Katrina asked me what I felt and saw next.

I can feel a pulling, not a pushing sensation. I'm experiencing many of the clichés we hear about ... entering a tunnel, which is brightly lit and hollow. At the end of the long tunnel is an incredibly bright white light. After a brief pause, I begin a rapid ascent, as if being sucked up with incredible force.

Moving at incredible speed, I'm getting closer and closer to the light as I shoot up the tunnel. It's becoming wider as I ascend. There is an intense feeling of love enveloping me. It's warm ... beautifully warm ... and eerily quiet. It's a lovely feeling. There are no sounds. I have no fear, only anticipation and curiosity for what resides on the other side of the light. I'm very close now. The layers I've been passing through contain different levels of brightness, where the intensity of the light increases as I pass through each level.

After a brief silence, Katrina prompted me to explain what I was seeing.

Drawing myself back from the experience enough to explain, I continue, *I feel my spirit self burst through the light. On the other side of it, I'm a little disoriented. Everything is bright white. It's clear I'm not in outer space; rather, I'm in a totally different dimension. It feels like I've arrived home.*

Katrina whispered softy, "You've likely just passed from the Earth plane to a spiritual plane. What else do you see?"

Nothing appears to be solid, I replied. *The lights vary in their level of brightness and density, although there are no colors other than varying shades of white. Also, there are no sharp edges; rather, all of the edges are rounded, with no symmetry.*

There are no smells, tastes, or touch sensations. In the tunnel, there was no sound, but after bursting through the light, I can now hear faint sounds. It's more of a vibrational sound, a soft, steady humming sound, similar to the hum of high-voltage electrical wires. It's very soothing.

"Describe what else you see."

There are two floating energy masses coming toward me. They are similar in shape to me. Both are brightly illuminated.

"Do you recognize them?"

I paused for a moment before answering. *I can see them both morphing into human forms, as am I. I'm forming into my body as Taynay. One of the energy forms is morphing into Comba, and the other energy form is morphing into my spirit guide, who I recognize and call Sacha. An intense knowing is flooding my consciousness. Sacha is an ancient and highly evolved soul who was incarnated with me many lifetimes ago as my older brother. Now Sacha serves as my spirit guide and appears to me in a male form, although like all spirits, we are neither male nor female.*

Both are communicating with me telepathically. We are sending images and thoughts back and forth between the three of us. They are telling me everything is okay and that we are temporarily taking human forms to ease recognition and transition from the physical world. They want me to know I'm home now and that I will be joined with the other members of our soul group soon. I let them know I understand and am happy to be home.

Comba's spirit self is giving me a long, heartfelt hug. She is communicating a private message to me, which can only be sent through touch. All telepathic thoughts can be seen by Sacha or other beings, but not messages via touch. Her private message is that she loves me unconditionally, is happy I'm home, and soon, she hopes we will begin planning our next life together. Comba's spirit self did not join me in my incarnation on Earth as Binh.

While Comba's spirit self is hugging me, other members of our soul tribe are beginning to move toward the three of us from a distance. I can see Samuele arriving, one of our children from our life in Italy as Allesandra and Peitro. My mother, Tien, from my most recent life as Binh, has also arrived. I can also see Anthony, one of the slave owners from our life in Alabama. Anthony was one of the white men who beat me mercilessly that day on the plantation when I was begging for them to get Comba a doctor. Oddly, I feel nothing but love for Anthony and all of the members of the greeting party.

After a brief time of welcoming, the souls disperse and I'm left alone with Sacha. We begin to fly across an incredibly vast distance, and Sacha is letting me know he would like to begin sharing karmic truths with me while we fly.

Telepathically, he is telling me that every life leaves an imprint on the soul, including my most recent life as Binh. Karmic residue from past lives carries over into future lives. He is telling me that residue can be seen on physical bodies in the form of birthmarks, which often are the exact spots of mortal wounds from prior lives. Also, medical conditions such as asthma and phobias such as an intense fear of heights can be caused by left-over residue from past lives.

Sacha is explaining that everything in the universe is comprised of vibrational energy and that great scientists such as Einstein discovered that all matter is comprised entirely of energy. By its very nature, energy cannot die; rather, it simply transforms. We are all just energy, vibrating at different frequencies, whether we are in human form or spirit form.

It's clear that Sacha prefers to teach through analogies. He asks me to view my true essence, my soul, as a never-ending life-force that simply changes form ... from spirit to human, and back ... just as water changes from ice to liquid to steam.

He is communicating that as we learn karmic lessons, we grow spiritually and become more in harmony with the universe. This raises the vibrational frequency of our energy. We are all part of one massive energy field, and because of this "oneness," the degree that our actions are in harmony or disharmony with the universe impacts the collective energy fields of all. He has so much more to share with me, he says.

"What happens next?" whispered Katrina.

Sacha is telling me I am about to go through a transition process that will prepare me for my next incarnation. The process helps cleanse my soul and allows me to let go of any leftover negative energy from my life as Binh.

We will soon begin the process of conducting a review of my life that just ended. We will focus on how my life played out relative to the initial life plan and the karmic lessons I wanted to experience.

"See if you can skip to the life review. Where does it take place, and who is there? Also, without going into too much detail on Binh's life, what are you seeing?"

I paused for a moment to see the life review before I began. *After a period of blank images, we are floating in a theater-like environment with several large flat screens, presumably to ease transition. Right now, it's just Sacha and my spirit self. We can see all of the major events of my* life as Binh on the screens. We're exploring the memories with the deepest emotional intensity. Sacha and I are discussing the major accomplishments and relationships I had. We're also discussing the missed opportunities and the destiny points that didn't come to fruition. It's a period of intense self-examination. Sacha shares a peek at the roads not taken and the adventures not experienced.

It was interesting to see how my life as Binh could have been different had I made alternate choices, although I was feeling no sense of regret, no sense of judgment.

As part of the process, my life review can be shared with other members of my soul group, and vice versa. For now, only Sacha is involved. My life as Binh is viewed in context with all of the other lives I've lived. Additionally, through my conversation with Sacha, I start to formulate some early thoughts on what my next life plan could include. Sacha is telling me that later, we'll have more time to view "glimpses" of potential life plans for my next incarnation.

This definitely isn't what I expected the spirit world to be comprised of. In my body as Nick, as a Christian, I thought heaven was a place patterned after Earth, to relax for eternity. This is much more regimented and purposeful than expected.

"Let's continue with the progression of events in your period between lives. What happens next?" Katrina asked.

Following the life review, Sacha and I are reunited with my soul group members, those that greeted us initially, as well as those that weren't part of the initial greeting. None are in human form, but I can tell who is who. All of the souls present are in the form of brightly lit energy masses that appear vapor-like. I'm sensing that some souls in our group are currently incarnated on Earth and are not fully present in the spirit world.

Sacha is reminding me that our soul group is comprised of like-minded souls, who have common objectives for soul growth. Once a soul group is formed, we are together for our entire period of spiritual growth, which lasts several thousands of Earth years. We incarnate together over and over again, experiencing destiny points and life plans as spouses, lovers, relatives, friends, and acquaintances. I can tell we are all at similar levels of spiritual maturity with some of us progressing slightly faster or slower than the others.

After an extensive period of rest, reflection, and energy rejuvenation, Sacha begins telling me the next step in the process involves selecting a body, potential karmic lessons to be experienced, soul mates to incarnate with, and our pre-arranged destiny points. It's called the life-selection step, and it begins with incredible promise and potential.

Katrina, clearly experienced with overseeing a between-life regression, seemed to know exactly the right questions to ask.

"Nick, can you stay in the spirit world as long as you would like, or do you have to reincarnate immediately?"

Sacha says we all have choices, I tell her. In some of my prior times in the spirit world, hundreds of Earth years have passed, while other periods in the spirit world have been relatively short. It's up to me. This between-life period will be fairly short in Earth years. I'm ready to go back soon, as my life as Binh was short. I have several karmic lessons I want to explore in my next incarnation.

Next, Sacha and I travel to an area that has a huge 360-degree cylindrical screen that encircles us, rather than the flat theater-like screens we used for the life review. Our position is in the middle area surrounded by the screen, thirty or so feet away on all sides. We are here to begin the process of reviewing potential life options for my next incarnation. Each of my thoughts is converted into images on different areas of the screen instantaneously. I'm sensing at this very moment, I'll be making important decisions.

"What are you seeing, Nick?"

Initially, all of the previous life reviews I've completed are visible. All eighteen lives are occurring simultaneously, and each has a section on the screen. I can see with 360 degree vision.

There is no such thing as time, no sequence of events. I can be anywhere and everywhere at the same instant. I can see everything pertaining to all of my past lives ... my births, deaths, thoughts, and actions.

Sacha and I telepathically discuss the two lessons that I've yet to fully experience or learn. These include, first, learning to love unconditionally, and second, learning to break free of attachments.

After much discussion, these are the two primary karmic lessons this next life will focus on. Several of my prior lives have focused on these lessons. I've made progress on loving unconditionally but still have more to learn on this concept. Unconditional love is the purest and highest form of vibrational energy, he tells me.

I've made very little progress on breaking free of attachments, as this is one of the most difficult lessons to master. Sacha is trying to help my spirit self understand that this involves so much more than just being free of material wants and involves "waking up" to the idea that we don't experience a feeling of completeness from "outside" vices such as money, sex, and success.

Much of what I've experienced in prior lives has failed to put down roots in the form of spiritual learning. Several lives have involved me aimlessly wandering, repeating the same mistakes and never stopping to ask "Why am I even here?"

As we begin discussing various life alternatives, images instantly appear on the screen that precisely mirror my thoughts. The images appearing are glimpses of different options, essentially different bodies that will be born soon. I'm able to process all of the imagery and multiple alternatives simultaneously. There are so many possibilities and alternatives, the challenge is to begin to narrow the options.

I have the capability to move the age of the body for each of the alternative lives forward or backward with incredible ease. All I need to do is put energy behind it, and virtually any aspect of dozens of lives appear simultaneously.

There are a handful of potential bodies that are of interest. Sacha encourages me to "jump" onto the two-dimensional screen in a body that will be born in Santiago, Chile. Suddenly, I'm inside the body in a three-dimensional scene that just seconds ago was on the two-dimensional screen. While in the body, I can move the life timeline forward or backward.

I can feel the aliveness in the body. It is incredibly real and warm inside the body. I'm seeing how the life in Chile *could play out, but it involves only glimpses of my parents, my health, my career, and key destiny points with various members of our soul group. I also transport my spirit self into two other bodies, including my current body as Nick.*

Sacha is reminding me we still have free will and that the glimpses I'm seeing for each life are only one set of possibilities that can occur.

Katrina said, "Okay, go to the moment of your life selection. What are you seeing?"

I've decided to incarnate into the fetus that will soon be born as Nick Dalton, son of Bill and Tracy Dalton. Sacha is telling my spirit self that part of Nick's life is purposely being veiled. We agree to focus on two main karmic lessons in my life as Nick: unconditional love and being free from attachments/outcomes. My challenge is to learn from life experiences and grow spiritually from the self-discovery.

Sacha is telling me that perhaps the best way to describe a life plan is for us to think of Nick's life as a connected set of interstate highways. Imagine planning a trip from Los Angeles to Boston. There are several alternate routes to take. A northern route could be LA to Chicago to Boston. A more southern route could be LA to St. Louis to Boston. The scenery, the weather, the gas station attendants we interact with, the hotels we stay at would be completely different on the two trips. In this case, the start point and the end point are the same; only the path to get there is different. Each path has a different energetic strength associated with it. We still have free will but tend to follow the path that has the most energy associated with it.

Sometimes our lives don't follow anywhere close to our most energetic path. Sometimes we end up completely detoured and never make it to Boston. For example, instead of following the route from LA to Boston, suppose as we arrive in Las Vegas … and then don't follow our plan to head northeast toward Boston … and instead begin heading southeast toward Houston. Of course, the end destination, or life, in this metaphor, is completely different. Sometimes a life follows a much weaker energetic path and takes a completely different course, he tells me.

"Nick, ask Sacha if your life as Nick has been following its most energetic path so far."

He is telling my spirit self that I'm on a much weaker path than my life plan called for. The life paths that are most energetic and preferred are populated with synchronistic events to help guide us to the right path.

Synchronicity and intuition are essentially a cosmic global positioning system, communicating with us to "re-route" to our most energetic path. The voice speaking to us via intuition and serendipity is often our spirit guide.

He is telling me I've missed several synchronistic signs at key destiny points. These misses have led me down my current path ... I ignored the "coincidences" and gut feelings. Our task is to follow the signs and interpret the clues left for us, he says.

At current course, current speed, my life as Nick will end with minimal spiritual progress. Essentially, I exited at Las Vegas and am heading south to Houston instead of north to Boston.

"Ask him about a key destiny point you missed. What can he tell you about it?" Katrina suggested.

Under hypnosis, I, as Nick, had been viewing my spirit self asking Sacha questions. When my spirit self asked about the destiny point, Sacha chose not to respond to my spirit self in the viewing area. Rather he chose to respond directly to me, as Nick, bypassing my spirit self in the spirit world to talk to me on the couch. He is specifically veiling the missed destiny point from my spirit self, as he does not want him to see this destiny point prior to incarnating as Nick. The visions I had been seeing of my spirit self in the spirit world went completely blank.

A new set of images began to appear directly into my field of vision as Nick.

"Ohhhh God," I gasped once the first image appeared. I knew that what was about to follow was going to hurt ... a lot.

Destiny Points

Some part of my mind heard Katrina sit up and recognized that she was straightening her back. Intensely, Katrina said with more force than usual, "You seem distressed. Do you want me to take you out of the scene you are viewing?"

Katrina's words sounded distant and muffled, as if she were in another room. I didn't respond and her presence began to fade out. I was completely focused on the images Sacha was communicating directly with me. The conversation between Sacha and me was being cloaked from my spirit self in the spirit world. Sacha was showing me scenes from the night before my graduation at Michigan.

More images appeared … It was a hot, muggy Friday night in late May. Earlier that week, I'd successfully completed my last final exam, and I was filled with optimism about the future, graduating with a nearly perfect 3.9 GPA, resulting from four years of obsessive type A behavior. I couldn't wait to start the next chapter of my life. But before this chapter was closed, there was still one last night in Ann Arbor.

The evening started with six o'clock dinner at a local favorite with my parents and grandparents. Following dinner, I met up with Jeffrey, Eric, and a large group of friends and we went bar-hopping. It was our last night in Ann Arbor, and it was glorious. Filling the air were feelings of nostalgia and a "knowing" that a chapter in our lives was coming to an end. This would likely be the last night we would ever see many of our friends and we intended to go out with a bang. Our gang met up at one of our favorite bars in Ann Arbor at 7:30 and planned to make it an epic night of drinking and remembering the great times at Michigan. It was a special night, and we knew it.

By 9:30, we'd started bar-hopping, ultimately settling on a bar with a huge beer garden packed with people from wall to wall. The beer line was taking forever. It's a well-known fact at most college bars, if the bartenders are male, then women tend to get served quite a bit faster. As luck would have it, most of the beer garden bartenders were guys. I'd finally got to the front of the line. I'd been ignored for ten minutes ardently holding out a twenty-dollar bill to signal I wanted to buy some drinks.

The images from that evening continued to flow into my mind. The tall, lanky bartender with his maize-and-blue Michigan cap on backwards walked past me for the umpteenth time to serve the girl next to me. She yelled out her order for three vodka cranberries over the loud continuous roar of the beer garden. She then turned to me with a smile and an expectant look and said to the bartender, "And this guy is having ...?"

I stood there, blankly staring for a moment, which prompted a curious look from her, followed by a confused laugh. Her laugh broke my trancelike stare, and I responded with a loud "three Bud Lights" to the bartender. Then the girl turned away for a second and then looked back … smiling.

Oh my God, it's the same unique and unforgettable smile that Comba and Allesandra flashed to me in prior lives, the grin where she looks away for a split second and then looks back at me smiling.

The mannerisms and facial expressions … the exact same tilt of her head at the exact same angle … the inviting yet direct eye contact … the same split of her lips that revealed her white teeth … finished with a confident adjustment to her jaw line. Her intriguing smile and overall look gave me the impression she had no idea how beautiful she was.

I gave her a warm hug for helping me out. She said her name was Lindsay … Lindsay Kline. We began chatting, both seniors on our last night of college. She had long, golden-blonde hair that curled on the sides. She was 5'4", toned, and well-built … likely an athlete at some point in her life.

Her wide green eyes were inviting and her most noticeable feature. She had a slightly larger forehead than most and a strong rounded jawline. She wore little makeup, except lipstick. Her lips were full, perfect for kissing, and her laugh had a Southern taste to it, like sweet tea, I thought.

For years, she had probably been considered cute, but now she was rapidly evolving into a beautiful woman, not the kind of tall, buxom girl that turns heads like Janice. Rather, Lindsay had a fresh look, with girl-next-door good looks.

"You seem familiar. Have we met before?" she asked me, as she repositioned strands of blonde hair behind her left ear. She was making direct eye contact while she talked, tilting her head upward to meet my gaze.

I caught myself thinking, there are over five hundred people in the beer garden. *What is it about Lindsay? ... I can't take my eyes off her.* I could feel her unique look swimming in my head.

"Hmmm. I can't place where we've met, but I sense the familiarity also ... just can't place it," I said.

I had a full view of her now. Her breasts were nicely sized ... more than a handful. I couldn't help but notice her hips moving side to side, as she turned and glided through the maze of highly intoxicated classmates. At the exact moment my eyes were admiring her rather curvy backside, Lindsay turned around with a friendly smile and asked me to keep following her. Teasingly looking down to her left and then up again ... she could feel my eyes on her, and she approved.

Who was this woman? I'd known her for fewer than two minutes and was captivated by her.

Accenting her golden hair was a noticeable lock of hair, highlighted bright pink. She confided in me that yesterday, for the first time in her life, she'd had colored highlights added in her hair ... for no particular reason, just a "gut feel" to do it. I remember, in retrospect, that she'd reminded me a bit of Reese Witherspoon ... high cheekbones and radiant skin, innocent-looking with a friendly, inviting presence.

There was instant chemistry and a clear familiarity for both of us. I'd never been so quickly drawn to a woman as I was with Lindsay. With a single glance and well-timed smile, I felt a unique sense of connection. I was drawn to her by a curious pull, as if we had magnetically been brought together, once in close proximity. It was recognition at the soul level ... but at the human level, we failed to recognize ourselves as two soul mates brushing up against each other.

We spent nearly all night tucked away in our little corner of the beer garden, ignoring everyone else around us. At some point, Eric walked over to chat. I gave him the wave-off and Lindsay and I never saw him or my friends the rest of the night. The same went for Lindsay's friends. The conversation was at times electric and at times profound. My body felt light … and my mind more alert than ever before.

"Fly Like an Eagle" by The Steve Miller Band played loudly over the beer garden speakers. She raised her arms above her head and began to seductively dance. Something was stirring inside me, but I wasn't quite sure what "it" was.

"Nick, I love this song. Sing it with me," she said. Using her bottle as a microphone, we began a silly duet and openly flirted with each other.

As the night went on, I felt safe with her. Safe enough that I could tell her my darkest secrets and ugliest insecurities. I was totally open with her, defenses completely down as our delicate bond began to form. There was no need to play the usual games or to pursue an agenda with her. Everything was authentic … and refreshingly real. I believe she felt the same way too.

We told each other our life stories and discussed our post-college dreams. Her philosophies on life, failed relationships, sex, and sports were bursting with life. We had our whole lives in front of us. We wore hope like a comfortable pair of jeans.

I shared with Lindsay that I was still dating Sonia, a leggy redhead I'd dated off and on throughout my senior year. Sonia had already left for home, as her finals were completed four days ago. Although we had yet to have "the talk," I knew the relationship with Sonia was going to come to an end once I'd gotten settled in Chicago, as Sonia was coming back next year for her final year at Michigan.

Tomorrow, following graduation, I was moving to Chicago to start a new job as an analyst at a top-tier investment banking firm. Lindsay was taking the summer off and going to Africa, to do volunteer work as part of a student volunteer program. She was excited to join the fight against the female sex trade there. Upon returning from Africa, she was starting a career in international marketing at a Fortune 500 company in household care products.

Reliving the conversation was somewhat haunting for me. I'd completely forgotten my apprehension about pursuing a career in investment banking.

We began talking about what we wanted to "give our life's work to." I'd gone through a grueling job search my senior year and had had several offers from the usual suspects that came to campus: I-banking firms, consulting firms, and big corporations.

I couldn't help but think I was settling for a prestigious and safe career rather than pursuing a calling.

I'd come to some definitive and idealistic conclusions about work in general that I began to share with her. "Lindsay, there are three types of work ... a job, a career, and a calling."

"Ohhh I can't wait to hear this ... Nick Dalton ... the purveyor of wisdom, the oracle of answers, and a legend in his own mind," she said with a chuckle.

I feigned mild protest. "Okay smartass, I was about to say something really thought-provoking. Maybe I should just keep it to myself?" I said, knowing all too well she was right. I did have a somewhat inflated opinion of myself.

"Okay, okay, let's hear it, oh wise one from Flint," she said. So I went into my speech about jobs, careers, and callings, the content of which had been inspired by endless conversations with my mentor, Reggie Tanner. He was a bit of a legend, having been CEO of a successful marketing firm for many years, eventually semi-retiring as an adjunct professor at Michigan. Reggie was a worldly man in his seventies. I'd learned more from him through our one-on-one chats than from all of my other professors combined.

"Aright, so as I was saying, a job is something you do to pay the bills. For a lot of people, the objective is to do as little work as possible for the maximum amount of money. There is no long-range career planning; it's just a job. Any passion and fulfillment in life generally come from outside of your job, which preferably doesn't interfere much with your personal life. A job can lead to a fine life, but we didn't go to Michigan to just get a job," I told her.

"You have a career when you take the long view of your work. You build up credentials, experience, and have a career path. There's an expectation that with progression, you earn more responsibility and compensation. You're a professional at your chosen field."

Seeing that she was listening intently, I continued, "You have a calling when you find work that is truly worthy to give your passion to ... something that matters and enriches the lives of others, in some large or small way. You find the work intrinsically fulfilling and don't make decisions based on prestige or advancement or compensation ... although if you are doing great work, those can often be side benefits of your chosen path. It doesn't matter whether it's Tuesday or Saturday; work is an integral part of your life ... where work and personal time can be equally fulfilling and comingled."

Reviewing the scene, I realized that there were so many non-verbal subtleties she sent me that I hadn't noticed fifteen years ago ... the occasional twirling of her hair, the way her eyes landed on me, the infectious smile, the signal to her friends to leave her alone with me. Perhaps if I'd met her later in life, when I had more wisdom and experience, I'd have recognized a once-in-a-lifetime love.

Lindsay and I were engaged in discussion about the boundless possibilities that awaited, and it excited us both like never before.

I continued to pontificate. "I'm not sure if any one of these is right or wrong, but for me, I want to find a calling. Unfortunately, I haven't found that yet, so I'm going straight for the money. If I'm really honest with myself, I've got serious reservations about I-banking."

All my idealism thrown right out the window for some extra oomph on the paycheck. It was hard to watch, knowing I'd betrayed myself and continued the betrayal every day for fifteen years.

Lindsay looked at me with a long questioning stare, and then with an odd mix of sadness and spunk asked, "What the heck, Nick? Why are you going to follow a career where you mindlessly crank out financial models for the next several years? Your choices aren't matching your ideals."

She kept probing, trying to get me to reconcile my plans with my high-and-mighty speech about finding a calling. Where was the societal value I'd be creating as an investment banker? Where were the lives I'd be changing?

I could see her mind working, openly questioning decisions she'd made months ago. Where were the lives she'd be changing promoting laundry detergent?

Prior to tonight, I don't think she'd ever really considered the difference between a career and a calling. She was curious and thirsty for new thinking.

We ended up talking for nearly four hours until the last call for drinks came at two AM. We decided to walk back to Lindsay's apartment and talk more. Although I was physically attracted to her, my mind wasn't focused on sex. I was mesmerized by this woman. I couldn't take my eyes off Lindsay, and was hanging on her every word. She'd left an indelible imprint on me. This lovely woman had infected me with her fun-loving smile, her wit, her provocative insights, her flirtations, and her veiled shyness. In a matter of hours, she'd penetrated me deeper than any woman before or since.

I wondered, why didn't our paths cross before tonight? We spent the rest of the night talking about everything and anything, eventually lying in her bed together, with my arms wrapped around her, her back to my chest, spooning. I'd undressed to my underwear and polo shirt, while she had added an oversized pink t-shirt to her sexy black thong.

When we faced each other in her bed, we gazed into each other's eyes as our hearts cautiously approached each other ... to see if they would welcome each other. I could see the dim light of the bedside lamp reflecting in her crystal green pupils. Normally, I turn away to avoid prolonged eye contact ... but not tonight. The mysterious connection was mesmerizing. I saw in her eyes something she was likely seeing in mine: the riddle of love at first sight.

I'd been waiting to kiss Lindsay since her first tease earlier at the beer garden. My heart was racing as I touched her cheek with the palm of my hand, guiding her eyes to mine. She moved her hand on top of my hand, offering slow, circular teasing touches with her fingertips. It was the only encouragement I needed.

As I leaned forward to kiss her, I could smell her lightly perfumed scent. Our lips met in perfect unison, as if we'd kissed a thousand times before. When her tongue touched mine, it offered the taste of hopeful beginnings. The sensual feelings awakened by my first kiss with her were pure pleasure ... something to be savored.

Normally, I'd be in a rush to strip her naked after seeing a pair of long erect nipples pointing through her t-shirt, but the smell, taste, and feel of her body left me with the curious feeling of wanting to hold her and caress her without cheapening the moment ... the most magical of moments that transcended my twenty-two-year-old body's desire for sex.

With her head comfortably resting in the natural curve of my right shoulder, we laid together, perfectly situated and silently entangled ... which I had no intention of polluting with words. Brilliant energy seemed to flow between us, transferring directly from her heart to mine and back to her in a circular flow, as if our hearts were lightly tethered. Throughout the night, we used our hands to lightly caress each other. It was a seminal opening of our hearts and an entirely new type of connection I'd never experienced before.

For that one and only moment in my life, I felt my soul intertwine with another. Two became one for a few fleeting hours. It was as though my soul had climbed out of a dark hole, only to catch a brief glimpse of freedom.

Then she whispered five simple words: "I like you Nick Dalton."

I'd heard stronger words before. The handful of "I love you's," from other women had always seemed somewhat disingenuous or premature.

But these words, "I like you Nick Dalton," penetrated several layers deeper than any had before or since. These words were unassailably real. These words mattered.

I swallowed hard. With a lump in my throat, I said, "I like you too Lindsay Kline. I've got a good feeling about you."

She stared into my eyes and ran her fingers through my hair, as if she were slowly caressing my soul and washing it clean for the first time. It felt as though she saw the world through my eyes. We fell asleep in each other's arms.

Little did I know at this most glorious of moments that I'd see Lindsay Kline only one more time.

Big Day Out

While I was still lying on the couch under hypnosis, Sacha continued to show me images from the weekend in Ann Arbor fifteen years ago.

At the end of the graduation ceremony on Saturday morning, I looked for Lindsay in the crowd of family, hugs, and flashing cameras. My desperately searching eyes fell on her ten rows back to the right. She was on her tiptoes, stretching her height, expectantly looking for someone. I wasn't sure if she was looking for me or perhaps her parents. Damn, I hoped it was me.

I walked through the barrage of folding chairs and chaos on the field at Michigan Stadium, the venue for graduation each year. She turned toward me, and our eyes met. I knew it was me she had been seeking when I saw her face light up.

We found my friends Jeffrey and Kurt, who were standing a few rows away. We had Jeffrey snap a few quick photos of us posing cheek to cheek with Lindsay's camera in the midst of the excitement.

I gazed into her crystal green eyes and was at a loss for words. My breathing was shallow as I looked up to the sun drenched sky, hoping to find something profound to say ...

anything. Her shy eyes were pleading, as we faced each other, holding each other's palms.

After taking a deep breath, Lindsay, as had become usual in our few hours together, was the first to speak, "Nick, I ... I just wanted to say last night was incredible ... unexpected. Why didn't our paths cross sooner?"

A deep wave of anxiety began to rush through my body. Everything was in slow motion. Still at a loss for words, I stammered, "I ... I don't know, Lindsay. Pretty remarkable, wasn't it? Damn, I wish we'd met as freshman. Who knows, maybe our paths will cross again."

She continued to look directly at me, expectantly waiting for me to say something else.

After a long pause, she looked at me deeply and said, "Who knows, Nick, maybe they will. Or perhaps ..."

After she took a large, deep breath in anticipation, her expectant eyes showed me that she longed for me to say something ... anything ... after the words "or perhaps" trailed off. Watching the scene from the couch fifteen years later, it was obvious she was opening the door for me to not let the previous night be our only night together. It was a moment when I let practicality overrule what my heart knew to be true ... a moment I would come to regret the rest of my life.

I hadn't explained to her that my relationship with Sonia was soon to be over. She didn't want to intrude on the fact that I already had a girlfriend. She was giving me a cautiously crafted opening to see if I would take it ... to confirm whether or not she was welcome in my life.

We stared into each other's eyes for several seconds, each taking a mental picture of the other's twenty-two-year-old face. It was as if we knew we may never see each other again. Those two words, "or perhaps," are haunting ... so fucking haunting.

I was frozen. All I could think to do was to hug and hold her tightly. Neither of us wanted to break the embrace. As her head rested on my shoulder, I couldn't help but wonder what her eyes were communicating.

While still under hypnosis, my senses were filled with the smell of her perfume and the feel of her long, flowing blonde hair brushing against the side of my head. God, it felt good to feel her again.

Then we faced each other and held our hands together. Her smiling face was contradicted by pleading eyes as she looked directly into mine. Lindsay then lowered her gaze and took another deep, hopeful breath. Her eyes lifted to mine one last time, giving everything away. Still holding my hands, she smiled and gave my palms a semi-firm squeeze and just let go.

As Lindsay turned and walked past me to find her parents, Jeffrey placed the camera in her distracted hands. I turned around to take one last look at her as she walked away. I saw her take a backward glance at me with eyes seemingly on the verge of watering. When our eyes met, she quickly turned away and within seconds, she had mixed into a sea of black caps and gowns.

How could I be so unsure of myself at this most crucial of moments? Why did I keep telling myself this wasn't practical because we would be on different sides of the world for the summer and different cities thereafter? In retrospect, it was fear. Fear of commitment. Fear of love withheld. Fear of crippling hurt … all seen through the eyes of a fucked up childhood.

Despite having just received a college degree, a milestone event in anyone's life, I felt a sudden and overwhelming wave of emptiness flood my body. I was physically weak. A cold chill ran through my every cell. I had thoughts of turning around to go find her in the crowd. At that very moment, I saw my parents and grandparents waving me over, from twenty feet away or so.

"Turn around. Turn around. Turn around," the little voice in my head was screaming. My intuition was in overdrive: "Turn THE FUCK around and go find her." My knees were weak. My heart was pounding out of my chest. I stood frozen for a few seconds, everything still in slow motion.

My distant gaze and temporary disorientation were snapped, though, as my family had walked over to me. My mother gave me a big hug and kissed me. She told me how proud they all were and that all along she knew I'd make something of myself.

I turned to look for Lindsay one more time, but she'd completely melted away into the crowd ... and just like that, she was gone.

Later that afternoon with my dad's help, I packed up a U-Haul and I was off to Chicago to start a new life. I decided to alter my route and drive by Lindsay's apartment. I thought maybe, just maybe, I would see her out front.

There was no one.

Lindsay was leaving for Africa on Monday. In the days that followed, I chalked up our unique chemistry to the intensity of meeting Lindsay on our last night in college. Rationalization at its worst.

That summer, her presence seemed to be with me dozens of times a day. Evenings were particularly difficult when I would go on long bike rides along Lake Michigan. Every time I went on a ride, I would obsessively think about our night together. She had climbed inside my heart and was burrowed in deeply.

After a couple of months, her smell and taste began to wear off, as did thoughts of staying in touch when she returned from her African adventure. Fear had returned ... fear of rejection. What if she'd already moved on ... or met someone else?

A few more months, and I'd lost from my memory the texture of her skin and the imprint of her chest when we'd hugged.

Still, throughout these early months, I wondered what Lindsay was doing at that exact moment ... particularly when I was out partying late at night with my new friends in Chicago. *Where was she? What was she doing? Had she become romantically involved with any of the other volunteers in Africa? When had she gotten back? Had she taken the consumer products job?* She was always there, lingering just below the surface of my thoughts.

By the end of the year, thoughts of missing Lindsay were continuing to fade from memory as my mind focused on my new job and meeting new friends in Chicago. I'd always been exceptionally good at compartmentalizing my emotions. Moreover, being young and single with a pocket full of cash in one of the great cities in the world was enough to keep my mind partially occupied.

I'd started to date and host women in my bed for the first time since arriving in Chicago. When I closed my eyes during sex with the other women that first year, I couldn't help but conjure up images of Lindsay. *What the hell was I doing? Was I trying to unwittingly "fuck her out of my memory?"*

In order to move on, I was trying anything to banish her sweet memory from my mind ... to make her memory not feel welcome with me anymore. From that moment forward, the prison I'd constructed around my heart would block anyone from getting inside. This, coupled with my dysfunctional childhood had given birth to "The Distance" ... my inability to open up ... The Distance that Kelly had spoken of years later when she said she could no longer date me.

By the end of my first year in Chicago, the inflection of Lindsay's laugh was harder to conjure up in my mind. After a couple of years, her unique facial features started to fade. At some point that I don't remember, I stopped looking for her as I walked through airports. Occasionally, I'd still see her in the faces of other women, but even that eventually faded away.

Sacha then began to explain to me what had occurred that last night in Ann Arbor. This had been a destiny point, a crossing of paths that had been pre-ordained ... an instant soul recognition that included intense chemistry and feelings of familiarity.

The strongest energetic path for Lindsay and I to follow was to fall in love. The path called for me to delay my trip to Chicago and spend Sunday with her, continuing our conversation. In the pre-Facebook and pre-texting era, we would exchange email addresses, which would ultimately lead to further communication. While she was off in the far lands of Africa, I would share my new Chicago phone number and we would begin talking on the phone and set up a date in Chicago once she returned to the states. This was to be the beginning of a beautiful lifelong love affair that would ultimately result in a marriage. Together, we would continue our extraordinary journey together, exploring our karmic lessons and life plans.

This destiny point slipped through my fingers, leaving only the crumbs that today comprise my depressing, confused life.

Our free will trumped the destiny point that morning on the field at Michigan Stadium. If either Lindsay or I had reached out just a tiny bit more at that moment ... that one decisive moment ... or found a way to find each other in the weeks or months that followed, then our most energetic path would have been restored.

Lindsay could have called the main line at my firm to find me after I started working. I could have searched for her, as well.

Sacha explained to me that though we had temporarily gotten away from our most energetic path, we could have easily navigated our way back and the blueprint would have been restored. Midcourse corrections and re-routing are commonplace.

I asked Sacha about the implications of following a less energetic path. He said these paths can be rewarding and challenging as well, but in many cases, will not include the key experiences and learnings set up in the primary blueprint. Rather, a secondary set of experiences and learnings are explored on the weaker path.

He went on to say that during the ensuing fifteen years since Michigan, I'd ignored several other synchronistic events and intuitions that would have led to chance meetings with Lindsay. Dammit!

Life Selection

Katrina had experienced instances before where a patient under hypnosis had ignored her questions and commands for several minutes. Based on slight body movements and fluttering's under my eyelids, she knew to leave me alone to my conversation with Sacha.

When my rapid eye movements had ceased, she said, "Nick, when you are ready for me to re-join you, just give me a signal and we'll continue."

Following the scenes in Ann Arbor, I spoke in a soft voice to Katrina that I was ready to continue. She asked me to re-join the life-selection process. "What are you seeing now, Nick?"

I began to explain that scenes are no longer blocked from my spirit self.

Sacha, my spirit self, and other soul tribe members, including Comba's spirit self, are all in the circle surrounded by the cylindrical screen. We're there to help each other evaluate alternatives.

Sacha telepathically downloaded a massive amount of information to us all. He's explaining that life selection is an iterative process. For those of us intending to incarnate together in the next life, we are here to build a blueprint for our lives. We select our bodies; set up our primary life outline; and choose converging destiny points, off ramps, and secondary outlines for spiritual growth. It's a process that involves extensive planning and creation of synchronicities that can guide us throughout our lives, if we pay attention to the cues.

It's now clear, in the case of Comba's spirit self and mine, that we will be incarnating as Nick Dalton and Lindsay Kline. We have a signal set up on how to recognize each other. As with all of our previous destiny points, she will wear something pink that is either unusual or highly noticeable. She will also adopt a specific type of smile that involves unique facial movements and a head tilt that will make her smile unique and recognizable to me.

Katrina asked what recognition signs I will use to help Lindsay recognize me.

I'll always feel the urge to give her a hug the first time we meet, even though it might feel socially inappropriate or awkward, given the nature of our first encounter. That specific hug, coupled with a verbal comment on how inviting her smile is, will help us with the soul recognition we burned into our consciousness. We should both feel an overwhelming feeling of harmony and mystery if all goes according to plan.

Sacha is reminding us that we place the recognition triggers into our soul memories to act as invisible, yet intelligent energy forces.

I'm realizing, as Nick, that creating a life blueprint is a highly complex undertaking, especially when one considers we arrive on Earth to advance spiritually, through learnings. Additionally, we have a part to play in other people's life blueprints. Our personalities will vary from lifetime to lifetime, although many of the same personality traits and character flaws will repeat until outgrown or overcome.

Katrina softly said, "Often, our soul mates will be the source of the most difficult tasks or karmic lessons, particularly for matters of the heart. It is through these relationships that we have the opportunity to grow the most." Then she paused for a moment and asked, "Can you take us to the process you go through to transition from the spirit world to being reborn on Earth as Nick?"

Prior to rebirth, I have one last talk with Sacha and with Lindsay's spirit self. I review my soul-recognition signs, my destiny points, and the synchronistic events that will lead me to my destiny points. I'm so excited for this next life as Nick.

I'm taken to a tunnel, similar to the one I experienced after dying, except it is dark rather than light at the end. I float into the tunnel and begin moving out of the spirit world, as rapidly as I came into the spirit world following my death. There is an intense sensation of warmth that envelopes me.

In short order, my soul is transported into a four-month-old fetus inside Tracy Dalton. In five months, I'll be born as Nick Dalton.

Before I went into the tunnel, Sacha explained that once inside the fetus, the soul and the developing brain will join and begin the process of forming a personality and ego. Consciousness will have then begun, which essentially is the melding of the fetus's physical brain with the soul. While in the womb, my soul still retains its memories from prior lives.

Following birth, the soul memories start fading. By the time kindergarten starts, most of my soul memories will have faded, except for the occasional déjà vu experience and the soul-recognition triggers embedded deep into my subconscious.

After my soul merged into Nick's fetus, everything went blank and images stopped appearing. Katrina then brought me to waking consciousness.

The entire experience was like drinking from a full-throttle fire hose: experiencing Binh's death; entering the spirit world; going through the life review and new life selection; setting up karmic lessons with soul mates, in addition to soul-recognition triggers; and then entering Nick's fetus.

"Nick, you're shaking. Are you okay?"

Instantly, I was brought back to reality. Looking around the office, it seemed strange to be sitting there. My voice quivering, I replied, "I don't know. My body is numb right now. I feel like I'm on the verge of hyperventilating and can't catch my breath. Fuck. My mind is racing uncontrollably."

Katrina handed me a bottle of water to try to help me relax, but she said nothing. We sat in silence for several minutes while I tried to gather my wits and pondered the knowledge that Lindsay Kline is my soul mate ... the one I've been in love with for hundreds of years.

Once I'd caught my breath and could put a coherent thought together, I said, "Tell me what you know about destiny points. I can't stop thinking about the sixteen hours on graduation weekend in Ann Arbor with Lindsay."

"Nick, destiny points among two soul mates ... it works like two powerful magnets in a large bucket of wood chips. Each time the bucket is shaken up, the magnets inexorably move closer together until they eventually meet. In the spirit world and on Earth, soul mates are essentially magnetized with similar vibrational frequencies. These draw attraction to each other and tirelessly seek to come together, while leaving other frequencies unnoticed. It's the process of like attracting like. It's the similar frequency that causes you to feel an immediate connection ... the 'rush' of hearts beating in unison."

I said, "Sacha suggested that when we take a route that is not our strongest energetic path, it's possible to then make a midcourse correction and get back on the path. What's been your experience? Is that possible?"

"Working with other clients, I've seen both sides of the coin. Karmic lessons, soul mate relationships, and energetic paths are incredibly complex phenomena that we still don't fully understand. The realities of our Earth lives also come into play. Years ago, I had a client in his early thirties who realized his soul mate was his best friend's wife. He'd secretly been in love with her for over ten years, but repressed it for obvious reasons. He had reason to believe she felt the same way, although neither had acted on it. This knowledge helped him understand why he had so many failed relationships and commitment problems with other women."

"What happened?" I asked.

"He decided not to tell her or his best friend what he knew to be true. He is still close to both of them and eventually married a life partner who is not part of his soul group.

He's aware of his soul lessons through our regression work and is working toward soul growth, just on a different energetic path. Honestly, it's a heartbreaking case."

She continued, "In other cases, reality constraints were less complex and soul mates were re-united. Sometimes a farewell is just a prelude to meeting again. Perhaps that's the case with you and Lindsay," she said as she smiled.

"Nick, in all seriousness, if you decide to seek out Lindsay, you need to carefully think through the possibilities of what you might find and what you plan to share with her."

Following additional discussions and a heartfelt goodbye hug from Katrina, I settled in my car and hit the call button on Ridge's string of texts. He picked up on the first ring. "Nick, we've got a serious problem on Thermster."

The One

"Ridge, I got your texts; what's going on? Please tell me it's not a disaster."

Uncharacteristically rushed and out of breath, Ridge said, "You better get down to the office as soon as possible. Colin and I are here now. All hell is about to break loose." Colin Dupree was the other partner at Cadwallader Smythe who was helping on the Thermster deal.

After I arrived at the office, Colin and Ridge informed me that during the preparation of presentation materials to be used on the investor road shows, Ridge had discovered potentially damaging information about Thermster. As investment bankers, we needed to ensure that the information provided to potential investors was credible and fairly represented the merits of the investment opportunity.

Ridge explained that when Thermster executives sent over their final wave of information to our ongoing information requests, everything had looked fine. Then he had received a PowerPoint document from an anonymous Hotmail account. The document indicated major problems with Thermster's ability to convert nonplastic trash into reliable energy, though all of the statements and signals the company had been putting out publicly and privately suggested the technology was fully operational and ready for mass rollout.

Thermster's technology for converting oil-based plastic waste into energy was well proven, but the fundamental investment thesis and future of the company was its ability to harness game-changing technology for nonplastic trash. If the information in the PowerPoint document were true, the entire IPO would be dead, which would hurt our reputation long-term and also have devastating near term financial consequences, as our firm only gets paid its fees if there is an IPO. We've sunk a massive amount of resources into the Thermster deal. Our firm would lose tens of millions, which would have crushing financial consequences for all of the partners, including me.

After a heated internal debate on what to do next, we called Robert Grimes, the managing partner of Cadwallader Smythe, a role that essentially acts as the CEO of the firm. Grimes is a short, muscular, eccentric type with a short temper, yet he possesses the ability to turn on incredible charm and could probably sell ice to Eskimos. Robert lights up the room with his presence, but not always in a positive way. Some, including me, would say he's a jackass.

After a short briefing on the phone, Robert understood the gravity of the situation and said he would return to Chicago that evening from his lake home in Wisconsin.

After we hung up, my cell began buzzing. It was Robert. "What the fuck?" he yelled through the phone. "We picked you to run the Thermster deal for a reason. You were supposed to be the best we got. How the fuck could this happen? God dammit, this is bullshit. I'm holding you personally accountable to solve this. You better get your shit together. I mean it, Nick." And then he hung up.

Ridge, Colin Dupree, and I all gathered in our oak-wooded board room on the fifty-sixth floor of our downtown Chicago offices later that evening. I stared out the windows overlooking the brightly lit city skyline. It was nine PM on a Saturday, and only the occasional cleaning person could be found walking the office hallways. Otherwise, it was eerily dark and unnaturally quiet ... like the calm before the storm.

Once Robert arrived, we reviewed the PowerPoint deck that had been anonymously sent to Ridge. The information contained on the eleven slides directly contradicted what key members of the management team had told us about the firm's ability to convert nonplastic trash into usable energy. It had enough detailed information that it could have only come from inside Thermster. It appeared to be a briefing document written by someone on the R&D team, but it was unclear who the intended audience was. The CEO and head of R&D had shared several documents and videos with us touting the commercial viability and operational readiness of the new technology.

Our firm was less than ten years old and we'd made a huge bet taking on the Thermster deal. This was our firm's first foray into the big leagues.

After internal debate and after having evaluated all of our potential options, Robert agreed with my recommendation to address this head-on. I would call Thermster's CEO Doug Rogan, on Sunday morning, to see what he knew about the eleven-page document.

Exhausted and drained, I arrived home at my condo and crashed into bed. For much of the night, I stared at the green numbers on my digital clock, but rather than hashing over the day's events, I found myself thinking about Lindsay Kline. The Darkness had been replaced with what I call The Wanting.

Where is she right now? Is she happily married? Does she have kids? Should I contact her? Would she remember me? If I shared my learning's about our special relationship, would she believe me? These and other thoughts flooded my mind, as getting sleep was hopeless, despite my emotional exhaustion.

I couldn't help but think how ironic it was that if it were not for The Darkness, I would have never gone to see Katrina nor learned about the true meaning of that night in Ann Arbor. It seemed as though a higher power had compelled the rediscovery of our special relationship ... synchronicity at its best. I committed to myself to pay attention to coincidences going forward.

Unable to sleep at four AM, I sat in bed with my iPad conducting Google searches on Lindsay Kline. Over two million hits, mostly profiling an Australian cricket player with the same name. I tried several other logical Google searches to narrow the search. After reviewing several hundred matches, I found that none were relevant to the Lindsay I was seeking. I searched LinkedIn and Facebook and found nothing relevant.

More questions dominated my mind ... complicated questions. *When we met again, would we feel the magic again ... the magic that spans lifetimes? What should I share and not share with her? If she's not in a relationship, should I pursue her romantically? What if she is in a relationship but not married?*

So many possibilities bounced around in my head. *Would her heart pick up on our special relationship? Or would her conscious mind dismiss me as just some guy she briefly met in college?*

I continued my cyber-searching throughout the day on Sunday and found nothing. I posted on my LinkedIn and Facebook pages a message: "Looking for a fellow Michigan alum from the class of '98 … Lindsay Kline. Message me if you know how I might contact her." No responses.

The logical part of my mind suggested she was married and had changed her last name, hence my inability to find her with Internet searches.

I decided to text or email all of the Michigan classmates I still had contact information for to see if they knew her or knew someone who might have her contact information. On Monday, I tried the University of Michigan to see if they had Lindsay's contact information. Surely for fundraising purposes, they had her information, but it proved to be just another dead end.

Despite the Thermster crisis at work, thoughts of Lindsay were consuming me … The Wanting I'd experienced when I first moved to Chicago was back.

Over the past two days, I had put in several calls to Doug Rogan, the CEO of Thermster. He usually was prompt in calling back, but it seemed obvious he was avoiding my calls. In the investment banking world, I'd earned a reputation as being highly aggressive but a very straight shooter who could be counted on to deliver results. In my original voicemail, I told him exactly why I was calling.

Throughout Monday, Lindsay was all I could think about. *Where was she? Was the catastrophic mistake I had made in Ann Arbor carved in granite or drawn in beach sand?*

Then it hit me like a gust of February wind off Lake Michigan. I remembered Lindsay telling me her life story on our special night. She was born and raised in Jackson, Mississippi. I had my assistant pull every listed phone number for the last name of Kline in the five-county Jackson area, which has a population of 539,000. The number of Klines was a manageable number, with seventy-one phone numbers listed under that last name. I just started calling.

There was no going back now. Throughout my life, I'd made a series of regrettable decisions. Deciding to contact Lindsay I hoped would not be one of them.

My script was simple. "Hi, my name is Nick Dalton. I'm trying to find a classmate of mine from the class of '98 at the University of Michigan. Her name is Lindsay Kline. Would you happen to know how I might get in touch with her?"

Systematically, I called all seventy-one numbers and talked with fourteen different Klines who lived near Jackson. None of whom knew her. I left messages for the rest. Another dead end, I thought.

The One

The next day, Tuesday, Robert Grimes went ballistic on our regularly scheduled weekly call on the Thermster deal. "How come we have not talked with Rogan by now? What the hell is going on? Nick, how could you be so fucking stupid as to tip him off to what you were calling about?"

In the midst of his phone tirade, I felt my iPhone buzzing. I recognized the 601 area code as one of the Jackson, Mississippi, area codes I had spent time calling the day before. I interrupted Grimes's tirade to let him know I had a call coming in that I need to take.

Grimes responded, "God dammit. It fucking better be Rogan."

As I was stepping out of the conference room into the hallway, my heart was racing. "Hi. This is Nick."

With a strong southern drawl, the female voice on the other end said, "Hello, Nick. This is Cheryl Kline. I'm returning your phone call from yesterday. I'm Lindsay's mom."

Feeling as though I'd been waiting for this very moment for fifteen years, I said, "Thanks for calling back, Cheryl. I'd like to get in touch with your daughter. We attended Michigan together, although we only knew each other for a couple of days there."

I was taken a bit by surprise and thought it odd when she said, "I remember Lindsay talking about you, Nick. Do you mind if I ask why you want to find her?"

"Well, it's going to sound a little crazy after so many years of no contact, but I'd like to talk with her. I'm not looking to intrude on her life or anything like that. I suppose I just want to see what she's been up to after all these years. I know it sounds odd, but if you would be kind enough to pass along her phone number, I'd appreciate it."

Her voice became softer, to the point where I could barely hear her. "Nick, I'm afraid I can't do that ..."

I suppose it was the unseemly "never take no" aspect of my personality that caused me to interrupt her in mid-sentence, in order to plead my case further. "I can appreciate that, but I really need to talk with Lindsay. I wouldn't have called you if I didn't think it was important. Please help me out."

Her voice turned from soft to clearly shaken. "As sure as I'm sitting here with a phone in my hand, I'd love for nothing more than to make that happen for you and for her, Nick. But I can't do that. You see ... Lindsay's dead."

As if I'd received a sucker punch to the gut, I felt my stomach drop right out of my body. A lump formed in my throat so large that I couldn't swallow. My legs turned to jelly, my knees so weak I got down on one knee, then two to steady myself. The twelve-by-twelve black and white marble tiles felt hard and cold.

Just as had happened at graduation, everything turned to slow motion. I simply could not speak, as there were no words in the black hole I'd just been thrown into. My body and mind were in a state of icy cold shock. I'd spent less than twenty-four hours knowing Lindsay Kline, yet I felt as though I'd just lost my one true love in a single horrific moment.

Where was this feeling of overwhelming love coming from, for an acquaintance I hadn't seen in fifteen years? Was this really love that carried through several lifetimes, or something different? Perhaps a self-delusional creation to mask my complete inability to feel true intimacy … my inability to open my heart to another woman?

I just sat there, unable to move. Clearly, this wasn't what I'd expected to find. Lindsay's death was a staggeringly decisive blow that struck me utterly powerless. Lindsay had entered into my life like a lightning strike, with no explanation why … and she exited with the same suddenness.

After what seemed like an eternity, I was still unable to speak. Cheryl gathered herself and said, "Lindsay died in an automobile accident. I'm sorry I can't help you, Nick." The phone went dead.

Melt Down

Through the glass walls in the conference room, Ridge saw me on the floor, with a pained look on my face. He jumped up and ran out to me. "Nick, what's wrong? Should I call an ambulance?"

Still disoriented, my mind far away, I muttered, "What? ... Wait ... No ... Don't call an ambulance."

Helping me up, he followed my slow and dazed walk to my office on the other side of the floor. He said nothing as we walked. Once settle in my chair, I said, "Thanks Ridge. Just leave me be for a bit ... and close the door."

"Jesus. Alright man, just let me know if you need anything," he said.

Sitting with my back facing away from the office door, I gazed out the windows from my fifty-sixth floor perch overlooking downtown Chicago. It was as if I'd fallen into a bone-chilling icy lake and emerged in a state of shock, shrouded in sopping-wet clothes. I was alone. So utterly alone in a city of three million people.

After thirty minutes of uninterrupted silence, I called the only person I knew who could provide support. I needed a sense of perspective. I'd never felt as close to a person as I felt toward Lindsay right now, despite our paths crossing so briefly.

Thank God Katrina picked up. Once in conversation, she said, "Nick, my best advice is for us to take the next few days and weeks to try to unravel what's really going on here.

"In your current state of grief, I don't expect you to hear everything I'm saying, but please try to hear me when I say this ... soul mates enter and exit our lives with very specific purposes. Maybe we'll never know why your two paths briefly crossed and then diverged. Maybe we'll never know why Lindsay died in a car accident, but you owe it to yourself to find out what you can about her life and see if there are any implications for your life."

She went on to say that sometimes events appear to be unbearably cruel, and the pain can be suffocating. Sometimes it is only after events fully play out that we begin to unravel the lessons we came here to learn.

A flash of insult and anger swept across me as she suggested that Lindsay's death could be part of some larger lesson. What a bunch of crap! I had to cut our call short. At that moment, I just couldn't listen to Katrina's babble.

Lindsay was dead. I hadn't even bothered to ask how long ago she'd died. *Had it been recent or many years ago?*

Had she passed in an instant, or had she suffered? Had she ever married or had children? What had she done with her life after leaving Michigan? Why had Cheryl said she remembered Lindsay talking about me after all these years?

So many unanswered questions. *Was it even my place to try to answer these and other questions? Would I be opening an old wound with her family if I inserted myself in any way?* The last thing I wanted to do was be intrusive to her family. Emotionally exhausted, I left work, went home, and crawled into bed.

The haunting green numbers on the clock I'd stared at so many times flowed into each other, one after another. Those fucking green numbers. The relentless feeling of fear had returned, as well as the crushing sensation on my chest. Physically, I could barely take a deep breath. The Darkness had slithered out if its cave to follow me under the bedcovers ... again.

For the next few hours my phone blew up with texts and calls. Possessing neither the energy nor the interest to answer calls from the office, I held the pillow tight and formed an imaginary cocoon. I pulled the sheets and blanket over my head and wept uncontrollably. The Darkness screamed inside my head ... "End this fucking life."

After six tormenting hours, I collapsed into sleep around midnight. When I awoke at five AM, I was in no shape to go into the office. Emotionally exhausted, I lay in bed for a few hours, unable to fall back to sleep. I texted my assistant Angela.

Not feeling well. Won't be in today. Turning my phone off. 8:31 AM

I received her response:

Bad day to be sick. Robert is back in the office, looking all over for you. He's pissed ... broke my stapler when he threw it against the wall. Thought you should know ... Angie 8:32 AM

For the next several hours, an internal battle raged in my mind. Thoughts and counter-thoughts raced at hyper speed in a tennis match of back-and-forth. *Who was it that I was talking with, discussing the same thoughts with myself over and over?*

The Darkness was playing the role of an invisible soul-eating cannibal. I just wanted the pain to stop and had an overwhelming desire to slowly drown in a murky bed of quicksand. It felt more appealing to sink than to try to keep my head above ground.

If I go away, would anyone really care or be hurt besides my parents? If it looked like an accident, maybe it wouldn't hurt them as much, I thought. I didn't want them to know I had given up ... and had chosen to leave them.

For the next several hours, I curled up in bed with my iPad, searching for creative ways to "leave" and make it look like an accident. At least it was something I could focus on, even if only for more than a few moments.

It was soothing to imagine my life gone, elegantly released from the world. Visions of my funeral suddenly became prominent. People would come ... relatives, coworkers, friends, Janice and her friends. They all would come and remember me ... just the good things about me. In a twisted way, it was incredibly appealing.

An accident would be best. Something that wouldn't hurt too much. Maybe an accidental overdose. It does happen. Maybe a single-car accident, perhaps crashing into a huge tree at high speed? Why couldn't God just make my heart stop?

Of course, my logical mind realized none of these were clean, nor certain to work. For hours, I carried on a conversation with myself, considering the possibilities and glorifying my funeral as a day when everyone would love me, even if just for that day. Over and over, I went through how the day would go.

My father would give the eulogy with my mother sitting in the front row, dressed in black, crying throughout. My colleagues from work would all talk about how hardworking and smart I was and how I'd accomplished so much at such a young age. Robert would likely blow off my funeral, like he had others.

Janice would cry and play the role as the devastated girlfriend in love. She would revel in the sympathy and attention from all of her friends, but deep down, she would say to herself that she had never come close to loving me, nor did she really know the real me ... just "The Distance" I'd created around my heart. She'd feel minor anguish for having cheated on me so many times. If timed perfectly, I'd kill myself on one of her weekends in Vegas or Miami when she was up to no good.

Some of the women I'd had relationships with would come. They would internally reminisce about the good times we'd shared, whether we'd dated or just had a short fling. Some would cry, while some would wonder what might have been had we stayed together. Most would say they never really knew me.

My ego was on an obsessive and perverted craze to garner sympathy. The dysfunction was breathtaking in its fanaticism. For hours, the fantasy of my funeral played in my head. Every detail, every permutation was considered. I knew all would feel something for me at that moment. I relished the idea of it, as my pain temporarily subsided.

In the midst of my mad fantasy, there was a loud banging on my door. I didn't answer. Another bang. Fuck!

"Nick ... it's Ridge ... I know you're in there. I need to talk to you. It's important."

I ignored the knocking, sitting quietly inside, being sure to not make another sound.

More knocking. "Nick. Please. It's really important. God dammit. If you're in there, open the fuck up."

After another minute of silence, I could hear a paper note slipped under the door onto the hardwood floor.

My energy level was totally drained and I couldn't muster the energy to get out of bed. For hours I just hid there, staring at the ceiling trying to sleep, not really caring what message the note contained.

Eventually, the urge to pee became unbearable, so I rolled out of bed to relieve myself. I then shuffled over to the front door, completely naked, to read Ridge's note.

> Call me day or night. Robert is going insane. The IPO is in trouble. Your entire career is at stake. Call me. Ridge

My stomach dropped, as a sense of further anxiety filled me. My mind began to uncontrollably race again. I couldn't find the energy to make my way back into bed.

I sat down on the floor near the front door. The wood floors delivered a dull, cold feeling. I eased down on my side but ultimately found it more comfortable to lie flat on my back. While staring aimlessly at the ceiling, I found it curious that I'd never noticed details before such as the multi-layered crown moldings or the shape of the light fixtures. I wondered how long I'd have to lie there before summoning the energy to crawl back into bed.

Eventually, my mind began to drift to Thermster. *What if Ridge is right? What if the IPO collapses?* It would be the lead story in the business section of every paper in the country for a day or two. The talking heads on CNBC and Fox Business would be all over it. Cadwallader Smythe would be irreparably damaged, and the firm's survival would be at risk. Fuck!

Nearly all of my wealth was tied up in partnership equity, which would be worthless if our firm were to crater. Moreover, I'd certainly be fired by Robert in a very public way. Doug Rogan would clearly be the face of the scandal, but within the blue-shoed investment banking circles, I'd be taking the fall along with Rogan. My reputation would be in tatters.

I was still several hundred thousand dollars underwater from the penthouse condo I'd bought just before the real estate collapse in 2008. It was bad timing to make a large real estate purchase. A meltdown at the firm and simultaneously being fired in a public way would be an utter financial disaster.

The Darkness was incessantly driving home the notion that everything was crumbling around me. Images of being fired began to flood my mind. I envisioned being in Robert's office, listening to him lecture about how my disappearing act on the Thermster deal had exasperated the crisis. This would be the reason for termination: I'd let everyone in the firm down and had to be fired.

There would be no severance. He would have HR "walk" me out of the office. They would ship my personal belongings to the condo a day or two later. The firm would be in damage-control mode, scapegoating me for anything that ultimately went wrong with the Thermster debacle. Gossip would be rampant among everyone who knew me: "Did you hear Nick Dalton screwed up the Thermster IPO and was fired? It's all over the news." I'd likely have a very hard time finding work in investment banking for quite a long time.

The life I'd built was slipping away in a desperate free fall. The foundation of my life, my identity as a wealthy, successful businessman was being ripped away. I was crawling out of my skin and didn't really know who Nick Dalton was anymore. I just wanted to go away.

As I lay there staring at the ceiling, thoughts of killing myself via a staged accident were replaced with making the pain stop "right fucking now," in this moment ... a decisive ending.

Could I do it? I silently asked myself. *Could I just end everything now? Do I really have the strength?*

I crawled into the bedroom, feeling every inch of the hard, cold floors on my bare knees and palms. I opened the nightstand drawer next to the bed and retrieved the bottles of Ambien and Grey Goose that had rested there for months. By the jiggle and weight of the bottles, there was plenty of each to do the job.

As I held the bottle of Ambien in my hand, my heart began to pound beyond its normal limits. The pounding was like nothing I'd ever experienced before. *Is this what a heart attack feels like? Ohhh God, please grant me this wish. Please make my heart stop.*

The physical pain was excruciating. I curled up in a cold, naked ball, desperately wanting the pain to stop.

Could this be a higher being, a God, granting me my selfish wish for a clean death? No pills and vodka cocktail needed. No note needed. Just a run-of-the-mill, over worked, over stressed investment banker dropping dead of a heart attack, albeit a relatively young victim of thirty-six.

At nearly two hundred beats a minute and accelerating, my heart felt like it was going to burst out of my body. The thumping was loud and violent. The pain in the middle left of my chest was severe. It radiated throughout my entire chest cavity from armpit to armpit. For several minutes, I simply couldn't move, paralyzed by the agony.

It was as if I had fallen into a deep, dark hole. I could feel my life energy draining out of my body via a dime-sized hole in my chest.

There was a mix of numbness in my torso and an intense energy starting to move up my spine. The energy was pulsating as it moved northward toward the back of my head.

Was this energy from my soul crying out to be released? My arms and hands were completely numb. Touching the hardwood floor, my body had no sensation of touch.

Breathing was becoming difficult. The unconscious, automated bodily function of inhaling oxygen was malfunctioning. With each breath, I desperately sucked air into my diaphragm and lungs and then exhaled. My breathing was shallow to the point that I could barely take in air. It was as though someone was trying to suffocate me with their hands over my mouth and nose.

While I struggled for every breath, the pain in my spine intensified. It felt as though hot liquid pulses of lava were slowly flowing up a small tube inside my spinal cord. The burning sensation was excruciating. I gave up trying to find a position to reduce the agony. Completely flat on the floor, afraid, eyes closed, writhing in pain, and barely able to breathe, I realized I was about to die from a crippling, massive heart attack.

Spiritual Experience

As I lay on the floor feeling close to death, images began to flood my head of a Blackhawks game Janice and I attended in the Stanley Cup finals. *Why were images appearing from a random hockey game the previous year?*

Viewing the scene, Janice looked stunning in her high heels, form fitting black leather pants and red sweater. During the night, she had turned more than a few heads at The United Center. I wondered if she still noticed all the double takes that had been so much a part of her life since coming into womanhood.

As was common for us at Blackhawks games, we had barely talked. Janice had been busy posting selfies on Facebook of our front-row seats along the glass. She'd spent most of the game responding to her friends' envious comments. The smug expression on her face conveyed satisfaction with the sixty-two "likes" she'd received.

By the end of the night, Janice had made sure that everyone who mattered knew she had two of the toughest-to-get tickets in Chicago. Of course, no one knew her enjoyment factor was close to zero because she despised all forms of sport, particularly hockey.

Meanwhile, I had been emailing and texting throughout the game and had been on the phone the entirety of both intermissions, obsessing about a deal we were pursuing. Work impinging on personal time is a dysfunction most investment bankers wear as a badge of honor. That night, Janice and I had been drowning in a sea of ego and we hadn't even known it.

Suddenly, from my view on the cold hard floor of my condo, our obsession with creating a false image for others was revealed to be utterly senseless. *Why had I lived life so foolishly?*

I was joined again by The Darkness and together, we stared into the face of death. I realized the fruitless searches for lasting happiness had always occurred outside of myself, while the true answers sat within and had always been there … but had been overshadowed by my focus on me, me, me.

By now, my body had been in excruciating pain for over forty-five minutes. The pain was paralyzing. I was unable to crawl to my cell phone to dial 911 and my breath was so shallow and wheezing that I couldn't scream for help.

Shortly after I accepted that I was going to die, my body became instantly still and relaxed. All noise in my head became quiet, like going from a Metallica rock concert to complete silence in a millisecond. My thundering heart rate began to slow, as thoughts decisively stopped flowing in. In the quiet stillness of my mind, there was an overwhelming sense of oneness, where everything was interconnected, like water in an extensive system of joined rivers and streams.

After a few minutes, I was able to stand and had an unshakeable urge to walk out to my fifty-third-floor balcony overlooking the city. Once there, I stood in complete awe of the mysteries of life, realizing the oneness of everything in my view. There was no separation, only a recognition of beauty and purpose of all things: the trees, Lake Michigan, people walking the streets ... all one.

Naked for all the world to see, I was never more at peace, freed from a dungeon and no longer a prisoner to the delusion that I was my mindbody ... that I was separate. Throughout my life, I'd been taught to stand out as an individual ... taught to compete against others for individual accomplishments ... taught to accept we're separate from each other ... taught to focus on accumulating and achieving ... rather than to focus on the collective good.

Following the most terrifying moment of my life, everything had changed. My awareness expanded in every direction. Colors were brighter, as if I'd gone through life watching a blurred 3D movie and then, at this very moment, put on 3D glasses for the first time. My vision was clearer, and sounds were crisper, as if they were coming from inside me.

I felt unconditional love for everything in my field of vision. There was a growing awareness that my ego, my prior self, was dissolving. To be more precise, my awareness was no longer confined to the limits of my body. Rather, my awareness was part of something bigger, in which my "localized" body was a center point for viewing the world around me.

I walked back into the condo and left Katrina a voicemail. "It's Nick. Know it's short notice. Really need to see you tonight. Please. Need your help. Call me."

My iPhone had blown up with backlogged texts, emails, and calls from earlier in the day. They could wait.

Later that evening, Katrina called. "Nick, got your message. Are you okay?"

"Don't know if I'm okay. I've always been afraid to actually do something self-destructive … until today. I found myself fantasizing about it. It's as if my mind was taken over, possessed by the demons in my head. And then something happened. I need to talk with you."

"Should I call someone to be over there right now and get you help?" she asked.

"No ... No ... I'd just like to talk with you tonight ... over coffee. I ... I just need to see you and talk with you," I said.

"Of course. Okay, there's a late-night diner. It's on State and Chestnut. It's walking distance from your place. Meet there in thirty-minutes?"

I was the first to arrive at the diner. The eight-block walk up State Street seemed to take mere seconds. With each step, I felt lighter. My sense of time was altered. I couldn't help but notice every stranger walking by and wondering what was going on in their lives. The college student waiting for the bus with headphones blaring, the elderly couple shuffling along arm in arm, the group of thirty-somethings exiting the restaurant. *Who are these people? What thoughts are running through their minds? What set of circumstances led them to be on State Street at this very moment?* I wondered. I felt as if I already knew them and felt love for them, as if they were a part of me ... part of my essence.

The pudgy short brunette hostess seated me in the corner booth I pointed her to, far away from any of the handful of patrons sporadically populating the diner.

When Katrina arrived a few minutes later, she was dressed in black as always, wearing her favorite red river stone necklace. She ordered a warm tea with honey, while I ordered a coffee.

Spiritual Experience

We skipped the usual chitchat as she asked me to describe in excruciating detail what had occurred over the past forty-eight hours.

I shared the earlier mental horror that had pulsed through my brain ... and then the euphoria I'd been experiencing for the past hour.

I tried as best I could to describe the sensory overload. "The coffee tastes different. It's more flavorful, and the temperature is more noticeable. The perfume the waitress is wearing is penetrating with every inhale. I'm noticing every minute detail around me. The fork has four ends rather than three. The clock mounted on the wall behind the breakfast bar is slightly over-rotated to the right, where the twelve is not perfectly on top. The floor is made from tan travertine with four differently sized shapes, all puzzled together perfectly to form an intricate pattern." I'd not consciously noticed the flooring in any restaurant I'd dined at before.

"There is an incredible sense of love for every person I've come into contact with since childhood. It's as if they're all amassed in my consciousness together, by the thousands, all there together ... and I feel love for every one of them."

Calmly sipping tea with both hands, she said, "After listening to you describe what you are feeling, I think you're having what I'd term a spiritual experience."

"Katrina, several sessions ago, you spoke about awakening from my sleepwalk through life. Is this a spiritual awakening? Am I awakening from the sleep?"

"No, I believe there is an important distinction between a spiritual experience and a spiritual awakening. There's a lot of confusion in this area. Spiritual experiences can be incredibly powerful, enlightening, magical experiences, but they tend to come and go."

She went on to explain that a spiritual awakening typically does not include an "experience," no matter how profound and magical it is. Rather, a spiritual awakening is a knowing ... an understanding ... a sense of "being aware of being aware."

No doubt she saw my eager concentration and befuddled look.

"You have no idea what I am talking about, do you Nick?" she asked as she smiled.

I said, "It's like you are talking gibberish. I hear the words, but they don't mean anything to me. 'Being aware of being aware' is vague. Let's keep trying ... Can you explain it a different way?"

"Okay. Let's try this. There are several types of spiritual experiences. Let me repeat, a spiritual experience is not the same as a spiritual awakening.

"One example of a spiritual experience is a 'heart opening.' This is when you experience staggering feelings of compassion and love for all living things. The feeling seems to come from a deep opening of the heart area on your body, often bringing about significant changes of awareness and heightened appreciation for life. Essentially, it's an energetic sensation of having your heart feel like it's actually opening to connect with the world. This is what I think you experienced earlier tonight.

"A second spiritual experience is a psychic opening. It's often paranormal. The person can temporarily see auras and will have insightful awareness about other people's lives. They might have visions of past or future events.

"A third one is a Kundalini experience. This involves an activation of an unusual form of energy, often starting in the base of the spine and flowing up through the spine toward the brain. Kundalini can result in meaningful changes in perspective and consciousness. Based on your description, you may have experienced some mild aspects of Kundalini.

"A fourth example is a drug-induced spiritual high. In some cases, the person experiencing the high will receive insights into their authentic self or glimpses of the world as its true essence ... energy vibrations."

She went on to explain that these are all mystical experiences, but none represent a spiritual awakening. They tend to come and go, transitory in nature ... a glimpse that fades away and soon, the person who experiences one of them is bounced back into his or her ordinary day-to-day life.

"Okay, I got it," I said, "So what's a spiritual awakening?"

"An awakening is a shift in awareness of who the self really is ... a shift from knowing yourself as a localized mindbody to knowing yourself as a limitless consciousness ... a complete reshaping of your awareness of who you really are. Nick, have you ever noticed there is a part of you that notices you are noticing? A part of you that talks to yourself?"

"Sure. Everyone has," I said.

Katrina seemed to take note of the definitiveness of my answer and said, "You have two selves: your egoic self, who is an imposter pretending to be the real you ... and a higher self, who is your true identity. An awakening can involve you getting in touch with the higher self side of you."

"More specifically, it can involve your higher self 'witnessing' your egoic side, which is self-absorbed in the day-to-day events of your life. It's from the vantage point of your higher self that you are aware of your egoic self.

Up to now, your egoic self is all you have known, Nick, but your higher self has been there all along ... kept hidden by the imposter.

"It's crucial to understand one person's awakening will not be like anyone else's, because each person is tuned into a unique vibrational frequency that makes that person's awakening unlike any other. But there are similarities that cut across most awakenings," she explained.

She went on to say, we all experience a form of awakening as a toddler. When the toddler recognizes himself or herself in a mirror for the first time, usually between the age of two and three, at that moment the toddler is "awake" for the first time that it's "me" in the mirror. The toddler becomes identified with the body for the first time. Prior to the moment when the child looked in the mirror, he or she didn't connect that it was his or her own reflection ... similar to cats who are unable to recognize their reflection.

We eventually realize the little body in the mirror is "who I am." We realize we have a name. Through daily life, the mind stores our accumulated experiences and a sense of self begins to be shaped and defined. As we continue to grow, the egoic side takes center stage and feels the need to protect me, me, me. We develop preferences, desires, relationships ... all of which create energy patterns that shape our lives.

I sat in the booth mesmerized, as Katrina continued her lecture. "Spiritual experiences like the one you had tonight *break* our identification with 'me' being a mindbody. This can ultimately bring a 'second awakening' to the universal truth that our true essence is not our mindbody.

"This second awakening affirms we're connected with everything. We are oneness. We are energy vibrating at a specific frequency connected with all other energy vibrations as part of one massive unified field of consciousness, where we're constantly evolving and affecting one another. Our true essence is not limited to our mindbody."

"At that moment, everything changes. You look like the same person, but you're forever altered. You stop seeking happiness for yourself; instead you seek happiness for others ... and by doing so ... you find peace and happiness for yourself. Isn't that fundamentally what we're all after?"

Katrina's tone was one of quiet confidence, and I knew that she believed these words with every fiber of her being. My coffee had gone cold as I listened intently. These beautiful truths had eluded me until now. Prior to meeting Katrina, I'd been unbothered by such important and existential questions.

"Nick, deep truths don't shout out to us, rather they whisper to us to come over and take a look for ourselves."

"Have you had a second awakening?" I asked, truly interested.

"Yes. I was thirty-one and had been experimenting with hallucinatory drugs, past life regressions, yogic practices, tantric sex, and various forms of transcendental meditation. I tried it all," she said.

She removed her glasses for effect and looked me straight in the eye. "Feelings of pointlessness had begun to consume me. I had an unbearable aching to 'find myself' since my mid-twenties and had become highly disillusioned. I could feel there was something deeper and more significant in me, but finding it had become an obsession and painfully elusive.

"And then I had an experience so utterly different that everything changed. It was as if I had been living inside a dark shell completely blind to what lay inside the shell with me. The experience I had ... it created a small crack, permitting a ray of light to shine inside ... the light of spiritual awakening. Eventually, I burst out of the restrictive shell altogether."

Overcome with curiosity, I prodded, "If you don't mind my asking, what was the experience that created the awakening?"

"Well, Nick ... I suppose you would appreciate this more than most. It was a sexual experience with a man in a hotel room that triggered it for me. I'll save the details for another time, though. Let's focus on you for tonight."

"Whoaaa. You can't just leave me hanging like that," I said.

With her usual smiling way, "Maybe someday when we're past all this and you're no longer a client, I'll share the details." Then, she deftly diverted the conversation back to the matter at hand.

I found it odd that I was able to put the images of Katrina having sex out of my mind, despite finding her highly attractive.

I was still struggling with the idea of witnessing myself and what the whole point of it is. "Even if we have an egoic self and a higher self, what's the point of it all?" I asked.

Continuing with a calm, confident tone, Katrina answered, "The purpose is simpler than you might think. Awakening causes us to overcome our sense of separateness from everyone else ... and realize we're part of something bigger than ourselves."

She twirled her glasses for a bit and then began to talk slowly, with deliberate emphasis on certain words. "We lose *all* of our impulses to worry about the day-to-day trivialities ... We *stop the cycle of feeling incomplete,* or of needing to feel more complete by acquiring money, status, and prestige ... We stop trying to find happiness *from outside circumstances rather than the inside.* When we break this cycle, we are on the path to living an awakened life based on *love rather than fear.*"

She took another sip of her tea and carefully observed my reaction to the words floating in the air. She paused for a moment to let what she'd just said sink in and then she continued, "We no longer fear not having enough or not being good enough. Low-frequency emotions such as jealousy, envy, anger, and sadness are largely impaired. It's a fundamental shift.

"The optical illusion called separateness is how you've been going through life, Nick ... it's the sleepwalk I spoke of weeks ago. The spiritual experience you had earlier tonight offered you a glimpse of what it's like to escape the un-awakened life. Your next step along this journey is to learn how to sustain your feelings of oneness."

Still somewhat confused, I said, "I still don't think I'm getting all this. How does this fit into having multiple past lives?"

She paused for a moment. "Think of it this way. We're like ocean waves, which can be viewed individually but ultimately the waves are part of one connected pool of water … waves that wash ashore and disappear back into the ocean, to later re-form into other individual waves. Do you see that each life is a wave?"

"Okay, I'm starting to get it," I said.

She continued, "I want to explore a little deeper how you've been living your life up to now, and talk about what causes you and others to be in a sleepwalk. Did you know humans are among the only species on the planet capable of thinking about the future? It's both a curse and a blessing for us. The curse is, we create *alternative realities* to compare against our current situation.

"For many people, these comparisons are the basis for emotional suffering. How many people spend their lives tying their happiness to some future event? When I get married I'll finally be happy … or When I retire I'll finally be happy … or When I win the lottery I'll finally be happy. These thoughts are all born from the ego."

She paused and looked at me, "I want you to try something, Nick. Try to clear your mind of all thoughts popping in for fifteen seconds. See if you can do it."

I rested both of my hands on the table and closed my eyes. Katrina was still observing me, silently sipping her tea. After several minutes of trying, I couldn't stop the internal chatter or random thoughts for more than a few seconds. Thoughts simply pushed their way in.

When I had indicated my failure, Katrina told me, "This little example shows how we've devolved to the point where egoic, compulsive thinking has hijacked our lives ... we constantly compare our current reality to how we think things should be. We're like the fish swimming in Lake Michigan. We're completely surrounded by water and don't even know it. Obsessive thinking is all we've ever known. To break the pattern, our higher self can observe our egoic thinking. By observing it, the madness is revealed."

Starting to understand, I said, "When you had your awakening, was it an instant moment that you never need to remind yourself of, or was it something you need to continually work at?"

"Following the initial moment of awakening," she replied, "I began to witness my life more frequently, without having to consciously think about it. Over time, I began to feel a deep sense of serenity, even in moments that would have previously caused me to stress out.

"Knowing that I live multiple lives and that humanity is one huge set of connected energy vibrations, I learned to let go of attachments and needing to be right," she continued. "I tend to float through life 'light and breezy,' and float 'gently down the stream' rather than thrashing around trying to swim faster. It becomes easier to laugh at good times and bad. I have more ideas, more flashes of creativity and inspiration. I live a more authentic life. My sense of personal struggle is over. I'm at peace with things, at peace with the present moment each day, whatever it brings.

"In my love life, I've learned to love unconditionally and at a much deeper level of intensity, but I'm not dependent on another person to complete me. Some relationships have been glorious and some haven't worked out. Again, I'm at peace with each outcome and learned from each person that came into my life."

Over two hours had passed while we sat and talked. The waitress slid the bill onto our table, causing us to notice the time.

"Where do I go from here?" I asked.

She replied, "Waking up is a process. For many people on the spiritual path, they spend the first half of their lives trying to form a healthy ego and then spend the second half trying to overcome the ego they've built up ... sort of like a caterpillar trying to overcome itself and morph into a butterfly. Nick, whether you like it or not, you're in the middle of the morphing process."

I nodded and asked for further guidance on where to go from here.

Spiritual Experience

After pondering my request, she said, "Whenever I'm in doubt on what to do next, I follow my intuition and watch for signs. Lindsay came back into your awareness for a reason. I would follow it."

Photo Album

Following the discussions at the diner, I went to bed with a better intellectual understanding of spiritual awakening, but I knew I'd seen only a glimpse of what was possible. I'd absorbed less than half of what she had said.

On Thursday morning, a loud pounding on my door woke me from a light sleep. The sun had yet to come up, although the dim light emanating from the surrounding high-rises was creeping into the room around the edges of my dark wooden blinds.

"Nick, its Ridge. If you're in there, please open up. We're all very worried about you."

I put on pajama bottoms and the first t-shirt I could find.

I opened the door and Ridge barged in, in his usual strident way. "Okay, truth is, we're not really worried for you. Robert sent me over here to let you know you have till Saturday nine AM to report back to work of 'sound body and mind' ... his words, not mine ... or you'll be fired for job abandonment. Nick, he's in a crazed rage, yelling at everyone he comes into contact with. Every other word is fuck or fucker ... he adds 'mother' to the mix whenever your name comes up."

Ridge went on the say that the Thermster deal was in crisis mode.

"I've only been out for one day. Is he fucking nuts? Anyway, is there anything new on the PowerPoint deck from the Hotmail account?" I asked.

"Ohhh, we're fucked. We had a call with Rogan last night. He reluctantly half-admitted the technology for converting nonplastic waste isn't anything close to advertised. Rogan tried the usual tap dance about how it's all fine, but we saw though his bullshit.

"Robert is personally taking over all the details on where we go from here. He flew out to Phoenix in the company jet overnight. He's in closed-door meetings with Rogan all day today. Colin mentioned Robert's plan is to 'put lipstick on the pig' and ram the IPO through."

"Ridge, there's no way this thing can go through without that technology," I said. "It's totally fucked. It could take the entire firm down if it goes bad. We should just cut our losses. What the hell is he thinking?"

"Hey, I'm just a lowly manager," Ridge said. "He doesn't give a shit what I think. Oh, and he is so pissed at you, I'm pretty sure he doesn't give a shit what you think either."

"Let Robert know I got his message."

"Alright, man. You know Nick, he's really gonna fuck you if you're not there on Saturday."

I hit the shower and decided to wait until after eight AM to call Cheryl Kline. I still had her number in my phone from her call earlier in the week.

Despite the chaos in my life, damn, the hot water felt good flowing onto the back of my neck and scalp as I pondered what to do next. I'd never noticed how soothing hot water felt when it hit my scalp, despite taking thousands of showers. I adjusted the shower head from my usual position of power spray to pulse then to mist and found myself noticing the different sensations from each setting. My mind traveled to a quiet place as falling water and steam drowned out all sense of sight and sound.

As the water rained down on my head, it formed a small stream on the back half of my neck, down my backside, also forming two separate streams overflowing the front of my shoulders and covering the front of my body. The streams of water seemed to have minds of their own, running down the backs of my legs and the front of my torso to the shower floor. God, it felt good. For a few brief moments, I was completely in the "now," without a care in the world.

Following the shower, I debated the merits of calling Cheryl Kline. I still couldn't get Lindsay out of my mind. Everywhere I'd gone since discovering our special relationship, she'd been in my thoughts: the office, the condo, cabs, and restaurants. Generally, I'd been immune from obsessively thinking about a woman ... until now.

She had completely infected my thoughts, just as she had fifteen years earlier. A wave of regret hung over me, as I knew The Wanting had an ache that could not be met. I sat at my breakfast bar, head in hands, contemplating the questions that filled my head.

With more than natural curiosity, I found myself in an unending game of speculation about the direction that Lindsay's life had taken following our time in Ann Arbor.

I planned to call Cheryl with no real game plan or expectations. I just wanted to talk with her, be totally authentic, and let the conversation just play out.

When she picked up, I said, "It's Nick Dalton again. Sorry about my behavior on our previous call. I'm incredibly sorry for your loss."

"It's okay, Nick," she replied with tired resignation. "Although I have to admit, I'm curious to know what possessed you to want to talk with Lindsay after all these years."

After an awkward pause, I replied with raw honesty, "Ummm, I've been going through some pretty rough times in my personal life lately. Been working with a therapist, exploring some of my past relationships and encounters with women. Anyway, the one night I'd met Lindsay ... the night before our graduation ... it may have been more of a profound meeting than I'd realized."

Not slowing down, for fear she'd hang up, I rushed into the next sentence. "There've been a series of serendipitous events that occurred which led me to re-examine our paths crossing, so I was reaching out to Lindsay with no agenda. I just wanted to re-connect, say hello, see if she even remembered me, and maybe catch up on the path her life's taken. Honestly, I was curious to learn what she'd been up to the last fifteen years. I know it sounds crazy, heck, it sounds crazy just hearing the words come out of my mouth. Anyway, that's it. That's all I wanted."

With what sounded like relief and reflection, Cheryl said, "Nick, you mentioned serendipity. My girl Lindsay used to talk about how we're all 'spoken to' by coincidences," as her words trailed off.

I said, "It's been a wild ride for me the past few months. Everything from a plane crash that triggered some deep-seated demons in me, then an unexpected phone call from a college friend ... that led me to therapy ... that led me to re-examine graduation weekend with Lindsay.

"I'm not even sure what I'm looking for. I feel a calling to learn more about Lindsay's life. I know it's a ridiculous thing to ask, and I'd understand if you said no ... but if I come down to Mississippi, would you be willing to have lunch with me and talk?"

After a long silence, she said somewhat hesitantly, "Well, it does seem a little odd, you wanting to come all the way down here to have lunch, but I do remember Lindsay talking about the night she met y'all ... and the impression you'd left on her."

We set lunch for the next day at her house. Excited, I booked a flight on Southwest, the only airline that flew direct from Chicago to Jackson.

I wasn't sure what I'd find as I boarded the plane the following morning at Midway Airport. I found it curious when the flight attendant announced that we were heading to the "city with soul," apparently Jackson's city motto.

After renting a car, I had a traffic-free twenty-minute drive to Cheryl's house, a one-story home with a modest Victorian look. The house was painted a steel blue color with decorative white trim adorning the old style covered porch.

The yard was well maintained and dotted with several large oak trees. The leaves had begun to turn yellow and had just started to fall en masse. A brick walkway led to a set of white steps.

After ringing the doorbell, I scanned the front yard and had visions of Lindsay in pigtails, as a little girl running around the front yard and playing tag with her friends, or setting up a stand on a hot summer day and charging a quarter for a Dixie cup full of lemonade.

Cheryl greeted me with a warm smile. "You must be Nick. Come on in and have a seat on the sofa."

The years had been kind to Cheryl. She was tall and had shoulder-length yellow-blonde hair that she likely colored to remove any hint of gray. She had the same green eyes as Lindsay, albeit flanked by late-fifties wrinkles that she kept partially hidden by a pair of fashionable black glasses. Her oval face was accentuated with high cheekbones, likely passed down through the generations. She was dressed professionally, with pearls, and a crimson dress obviously tailored to fit her shape perfectly.

After a moment of idle chit chat about my flight, Cheryl shared with me that she's a partner at a local marketing firm. She had taken the afternoon off from work to have lunch and chat with me.

She excused herself and disappeared into the kitchen. Her walls were adorned with pictures of her and her husband together throughout the years, as well as pictures of Lindsay in an array of poses: riding horseback as a little girl, overlooking the Grand Canyon on a family vacation, holding a fishing rod on the dock of a lake, and sitting in the cockpit of a small airplane.

I was completely mesmerized by the pictures, seeing the landscape of Lindsay's life in front of me from childhood through her teens to womanhood.

I'd forgotten some of the nuances of her unique look. For the past week, I'd had only mental pictures to fixate on, as I had no record of her. She'd entered and exited my life without a single trace.

Cheryl came out of the kitchen carrying a serving tray that included a pitcher of tea with two glasses of ice.

She gracefully sat down in a large brown leather chair across from me. "So, Nick, why don't you tell me a little bit about yourself and then we can chat about Lindsay."

The question unwittingly reminded me that the tapestry of my life was still being written, while Lindsay's story had ended. I went through the ten-minute version of my life story, hitting all the usual surface-level highlights: single child from Flint, high school athlete, first in my family to go to college, investment banker, living in Chicago, and never married.

Without a hint of hesitation, she asked why I was in counseling. No doubt, Cheryl was a strong woman, a woman of substance and not someone you'd want to trifle with, yet I found her presence to be inviting … her look, her demeanor, her inquisitiveness.

I felt at ease and able to open up to her. "I'm clinically depressed. Sometimes it's like I'm living someone else's life … all the disappointing relationships, the daily grind of building a career, and utter lack of fulfillment. Basically, I'm not happy with the way things are turning out for me. My personal life is a train wreck, every day a struggle. So I'm trying to find answers."

With gentle eyes, she said, "I appreciate your candor."

She walked over to the end table and picked up a large blue photo album, which weighed at least ten pounds. Cheryl held it close to her chest, almost as if she were caressing a newborn baby. She sat next to me on the couch and placed it on the antique walnut coffee table in front of us.

Filled with a deep sense of sadness, her voice was heavy as she said, "Memories and pictures are all I have left of my baby girl."

Photo Album

She'd organized the pictures chronologically. We viewed baby and toddler pictures. Damn Lindsay had been a cute kiddo. At each page Cheryl would tell me the story behind the pictures.

Lindsay was a bit of a tomboy as a child. She played all the sports: Little League baseball, soccer, and basketball on co-ed teams. Pictures of her with MVP trophies filled the scrapbook. She was the best athlete among her friends in Jackson and was also a nationally recognized figure skater. She'd made it to the Olympic trials in her sophomore year in high school, although she hadn't qualified.

Cheryl confided that Lindsay had been a typical kid in high school, not overly popular, as she had traveled a lot for skating. She had a small but stable group of friends that regularly appeared in her teenage adventures.

As we turned the pages of the photo album, I began to feel light physical sensations that mirrored the pictures we were viewing. I could feel a touch of cold brass on my fingertips as Lindsay posed holding a figure skating medal connected to a red, white, and blue ribbon draped around her neck. She'd just been awarded first place in a junior-level skating competition.

As we continued flipping through the pictures, the sensations began to intensify, and visions began to fill my head, as if Lindsay were forcing herself into my awareness.

The pictures were morphing into short vignettes in my head. I saw Lindsay starting the engine to her car and putting it in drive for the first time. I saw visions of her lugging a heavy TV into her freshman dorm room at Michigan. And so it went, a mental vignette with excruciating detail following each set of pictures.

We flipped through her college pictures. Her transformation from high school to college was significant. Gone were the braces and tomboyish look. She had grown into a beautiful woman. Her blonde hair had grown out, as had her shapely body.

There were pictures of her at many of the same events I'd attended. We'd unknowingly been at the same Michigan football and basketball games and some of the same special-guest lectures on campus. She lived only four blocks away from my apartment our junior year. How was it that our paths hadn't crossed until our last night in Ann Arbor?

When I turned to the next set of pictures, my heart started to pound and my hands began to tremble. There were three pictures of us on graduation morning on the field at Michigan Stadium ... the pictures Jeffrey had snapped with Lindsay's camera on that fateful morning.

It was as though a time machine were transporting me back to Ann Arbor. The feelings from that weekend began to flood my body ... a sustained rush caused by a re-uniting of our eternally linked soul energy. I could feel it now as clearly as I had fifteen years earlier.

Defenseless, I quietly pondered the catastrophic mistake of not turning around and pursuing Lindsay that morning. There we were, smiling cheek to cheek, with our black graduation caps tilted off to the sides of our heads. The second picture had several of us crowding in, making silly faces. Jeffrey had snapped a third picture that captured the brief moment of Lindsay and me hugging, our caps having fallen during our final embrace.

We were so young and hopeful, our faces were filled with pride, yet beneath it all laid an unassailable truth: this was a decisive moment on a most crucial day, in retrospect, perhaps the most crucial of days. One chapter was closing and a new one was opening. With crystal clarity, I could hear Lindsay's voice repeating those longing words "or perhaps ..."

Like an angry lead pipe crashing against my exposed kneecaps, it hit me. Lindsay was dead. All the dreams, all the hopes, all the future milestones of a life yet to be fully lived. All the thoughts that had filled her head that day ... gone.

I paused on the page for several minutes, staring without speaking, utterly broken down with grief. Tears crawled down my cheeks, drowning my penchant for hiding emotions. The Distance that I had put up around my heart all those years ago was toppled by these haunting pictures of us.

I did my best to recount for Cheryl how Lindsay and I had met in the beer garden and how we had stayed up all night talking.

"Cheryl, she touched me. She touched my heart like no one has before or since, breaking through all of my defenses. We shared our hopes, dreams, and fears. We kept most of our clothes on that night, but by baring our souls, we were naked to each other. In the months that followed, I often wondered if this chance meeting was our fate."

"Nick," Cheryl said gently, "people often remember details about milestones. I remember a lot about that weekend too. You probably don't know this, but you were all Lindsay could talk about at the graduation party at her apartment afterward. She'd been wearing a wide-eyed grin all morning and afternoon. Until that day, she'd been excited to go on her African adventure. When I asked her about the trip, she confided in me she was feeling regret. She wanted to spend more time with you. She wasn't sure what to do next. She mentioned you already had a girlfriend. Three months volunteering in Africa with a group of semi-strangers suddenly didn't seem so appealing."

Cheryl looked me in the eyes with a long, questioning look. "I'm curious ... Curious to know why you didn't reach out to her, or respond when Lindsay reached out to you when she got back from her trip. Lindsay assumed you didn't have the same feelings for her that she had for you. She was pretty disappointed when she never heard back."

The revelation was devastating, seemingly coming directly from the lips of a cruel and twisted fate. "What ... What are you talking about? I never received a message from Lindsay. She was all I could think about that summer. It was driving me crazy that she was in Africa and I had no way to get in touch with her. No ... I never received the message," shaking my head in disbelief.

"She told me she called your office and left a message that she wanted to come to Chicago and see you. She never heard back and assumed you were either in a relationship or weren't interested."

Fuuuuuck!

I silently slumped on the couch with a blank stare, wondering why circumstances had seemed to collude against us. We were supposed to be together. As I reflected on the crushing disappointment of not receiving Lindsay's message, I remembered traveling back and forth to Mexico for work at the end of that summer. I hadn't been in the office much. The message must have gotten lost in the shuffle somehow.

After a few agonizing moments of silence and reflection, Cheryl resumed commenting on the photos as we flipped through the huge album.

With each page we turned, it was as if a chapter in a mystery novel was being revealed. I was in no hurry, wanting to savor each moment of Lindsay's life.

After returning from Africa, Lindsay had rescinded her job acceptance from the consumer products company. She ended up cofounding a recruiting company that fall with some former members of the US Olympic Committee ... people she'd encountered in her skating days.

Her company focused on recruiting and placing former amateur Olympic athletes into new careers after their days of competition were over. She leveraged her knowledge of the void that is left for world-class athletes, who suddenly go from receiving massive adulation and ego stroking to being ordinary Joe's overnight. Her company eventually expanded to help returning and disabled military veterans find suitable careers after their service ended.

There was a picture of Lindsay and her two partners holding up a check from their first corporate client who hired athletes. There were pictures of ribbon-cutting ceremonies as the company grew from a small start-up to more than fifty employees. I could feel the black plastic-handled scissors in my right hand and the celebratory red ribbon in my left.

The next set of pictures included Lindsay with military veterans and former Olympic athletes, some of whom I recognized.

Cheryl told me, "I vaguely remember Lindsay talking about your 'calling' conversation ... when she told her dad and I that she was turning down her job offer. Nick, you influenced her more than you know. Your conversation with Lindsay was significant. It changed the trajectory of her life. She used to say that sometimes just a seemingly insignificant remark or occurrence can set off a chain reaction of remarkable coincidences."

Sitting up, I found the impact I'd left on Lindsay's life highly confusing. I had left an imprint that had permanency and could never be removed. This was a gift I'd unknowingly given her, and she had in turn passed it along to thousands of job seekers. *Was this a reason our paths had crossed? What imprint had she left on me? Was she leaving it now, after she'd already gone?*

I was brought back from my mental wanderings when, Cheryl said, "Lindsay said she felt lucky that she'd found her calling early in life. She used to shine every time she talked about how her company's mission was to make people's dreams come true every day. Nick, she got a 'high' talking about how her company made a job offer every twenty-six minutes."

As I scanned the pictures, I could see how accomplished and rewarding Lindsay's professional life had become. Cheryl confided in me that Lindsay's love life had been rather ordinary, though, filled mostly with high hopes and disappointments ... not dissimilar from mine, I suppose. There were various holiday and vacation pictures with different men throughout her twenties.

Eventually, we landed on a page full of engagement photos. With sad eyes, I viewed the pictures. She had been so beautiful and full of smiles ... smiles that weren't meant for me.

"Lindsay got engaged when she was thirty-two." The handful of pictures Cheryl had included in the photo album were breathtaking. Lindsay's fiancée, Andrew was an accomplished skier, on and off the US National Team over the years. Unfortunately, their engagement didn't lead to a wedding.

"Of course, she was devastated as things began to unravel. By the end, she was just relieved. Lindsay said it was a case of two good-hearted people who wanted to make things work, but couldn't. She said she loved Andrew, but wasn't "in love" with him. It just wasn't meant to be. It was a hard time for her, but ultimately she came out of it much stronger. Following the end of the engagement, Lindsay was a changed woman, like a burden was lifted. She seemed more confident and full of life. The devastation was short-lived and the old Lindsay was back ... the Lindsay who she believed she could do anything."

As we turned the page, an old crumpled steakhouse restaurant napkin appeared in the photo album. It contained a dozen or so handwritten bucket list items. Nearly half were scratched off as "accomplished." On the pages that followed, there were snapshots of Lindsay fulfilling her bucket list ... pictures of her visiting exotic locations in Australia, Bora Bora, and the Greek Isles with varying groups of friends. More pictures followed of her completing a one-hundred mile bike ride along the French Riviera and her participating in an African safari. Another of Lindsay holding a bartending license, something she had earned just for fun. She'd even completed a half-marathon, crossing the finish line hand-in-hand with her closest friend.

Lindsay had become a huge football fan over the years. The album contained photos of her hosting clients and friends at various Super Bowls and big-time college football games. There was a picture of her at a Notre

Dame game holding a funny sign saying "Rudy Was Offsides." She hated the Irish, along with every other Michigan alum.

She'd received her pilot's license and helicopter license in less than a year. The photo album had several aerial pictures of Lindsay flying helicopters all over the Southeast. She had continued to date men off and on for the remaining years of her life, but never married.

We were coming to the end of the photo album. There were only two pages of pictures left. A surreal feeling started to come over me. Cheryl and I had reviewed nearly all of Lindsay's life, all condensed into one book of photographs.

I wondered, *Is life really so trivial that an entire lifetime of dreams, accomplishments, insecurities, emotions, and relationships could be encapsulated in a single photo album?* My mind was flooded with thoughts of how we're all going to die. *What happens to all of the photographs and digital pictures? Where do they go? Will I be the keeper of my parents' most precious photos? What will I do with them? When I die, what will happen to their pictures and mine?* I figured, eventually most photographs end up incinerated, deleted, or in non-descript landfills.

The finality and seemingly meaningless nature of a life encapsulated by a photo album decomposing in a landfill was dreadful to me.

What was the purpose of Lindsay's life? What's the purpose of my life? Why do we come here? The big questions of life and death bombarded me, but no answers came. I was consumed with grief and angst as we approached the last few pictures.

We turned to the second-to-last page, which contained pictures from a concert outing that Lindsay had attended with a group of friends in Atlanta at Chastain Amphitheater, a quaint outdoor summer concert venue. The Steve Miller Band was playing that night. The last picture of Lindsay alive was one in which she and her friends were all singing along and striking poses. She was flashing the same smile that had stolen my heart in several lifetimes. I couldn't help but wonder if "Fly Like an Eagle" had been the song behind the sing-along. A song that had history for us.

At that moment, I wondered if Lindsay had even the slightest inkling this would be the last picture taken of her alive? She was stunning ... pure sunshine encapsulated in a photograph.

Cheryl clutched my hand, as if to silently acknowledge her understanding of the bond we shared in our love for

Lindsay. Visibly shaken and with tears running from both eyes, Cheryl said, "We retrieved these last set of pictures off her cell phone, which was provided to us by the hospital in Atlanta."

As I turned over the last page, I saw there were no pictures, just a laminated obituary from the *Atlanta Journal Constitution.*

There was a beautiful picture of Lindsay smiling, followed by standard obituary text underneath.

Through my red, tear-filled eyes, I read the words several times. Something didn't seem right.

July 17, 2014 …. July 17, 2014 …. July 17, 2014. Why was that date so prominent in my mind? … The day of the plane crash in Atlanta … the plane I was supposed to be on … the plane I missed because of a traffic jam caused by a car wreck on I-85 in downtown Atlanta.

I felt a shooting pain run from the base of my neck right to my temples. It was among the worst headaches I'd ever experienced … excruciating, pulsating pain.

My imagination intensified the pain, which was prolonged by the haunting images repeating over and over in my head of Lindsay's car wreck … images pounding my head like echoes in a chamber.

I needed to be alone with my thoughts. Following several minutes of pleasantries, Cheryl handed me the graduation picture of Lindsay and I hugging. She asked me to keep it. "Something to keep Lindsay in your memory," she said.

I thanked Cheryl and bid her goodbye ... knowing that I'd never be back.

Awakening

As I sat on the evening flight to Chicago on the half-empty airplane, I couldn't help but wonder ... *Was it Lindsay's misfortune that caused the traffic jam that fateful day, serendipity at its cruelest? A fulfilled soul contract between Lindsay and me that called for a plan B following a bungled life plan? Or just a sick, twisted coincidence of two unrelated events randomly converging at the same time?*

Was Lindsay, who reappeared in my life after her death, trying to nudge me in a completely different trajectory? I recalled Katrina telling me the reason for a soulful relationship wasn't often clear until it was already over ... like a delayed chemical reaction that ultimately transforms both lives.

Following takeoff and the usual flight attendant script over the intercom, I reflected on the afternoon spent with Cheryl. Eyes closed, I tried to recreate the feeling of warmth and relaxation from my sessions with Katrina by imagining the golden light surrounding my body. After I had spent a few minutes of applying her techniques, random thoughts stopped popping in my head as I reached a semi-meditative state.

Awakening

As I entered the quiet stillness, I sensed an outside force rising to meet me ... Sacha.

"Who am I?" I asked.

For much of my life, I'd been so absorbed in the day-to-day dramas that I'd been blind to asking the big questions in life. But, since my first regression, the world was beginning to look different.

As I sat comfortably in my seat, answers started to well up inside me. There was a massive upsurge of energy that pulsed throughout my body, accompanied by an overwhelming sense of knowing grander truths. Perhaps this was the "second great awakening" that Katrina had spoken of.

Knowings then flowed in. "You asked, Who am I?"

"You find 'who you are' by accepting that you're the awareness behind the thoughts ... You're not the thoughts ... You're the one watching the thoughts. Your mindbody is simply a vessel for you to live in the material world on Earth."

I sat quietly and "listened" to what Sacha had to say. "You're comprised of eternal energy vibrations, not skin and bones. All people, all things ... everything is energy, whose vibrational levels are perceived through the five senses. Equating the mindbody to who we are is the cause of endless suffering. Just look around and see people's collective anxiety about bodyweight, beauty, and financial insecurity.

"Your mindbody has constantly been in states of ease and unease, stress and relaxation, happy and unhappy, excited and bored ... what most people call normal. This is because your mindbody is unconscious to the fact that you never die."

"What is 'the it' that never dies?" I silently asked.

Sacha continued to provide answers. "You've noticed the red river colored stones on Katrina's necklace. Think of each stone as one of your individual lives and think of the gold neck chain connecting them as 'the it' that never dies ... the soul itself. More specifically, imagine one stone representing your life as Nick, which includes your role as a son, grandson, investment banker, boyfriend, friend ... the roles that comprise the 'human' side of you. Think of your soul as the 'being' that observes your human side. The two intertwine like Katrina's necklace to form 'human being.' It's the awareness of both dimensions and the toggling between the two ... the foreground and background, where the magic happens.

"When you accept the reality that you have a soul that never dies, the 'heaviness' of life will be lifted and you will enjoy more and stress less. The 'lightness' of your awareness will reveal itself. You'll let go of toxic emotions by viewing them through the lens that you are eternal, one with all, and here to learn lessons ... lessons that involve helping others and raising your vibrational frequency."

"How do I know if I'm on the right path?" I asked.

Sacha's insights continued to flood my mind. "I will directly intervene by sending you messages in the form of synchronicity ... mysterious coincidences. Synchronous events signify the intersection between your pre-life plan and your current life circumstances. These synchronicities are meant to gently nudge you back toward your pre-life plan. The key is to pay attention to the synchronicities and be honest about what they are saying to you. If you see a coincidence ... listen to it and consider following it Nick.

"You've constantly been given hints to watch for ... intuitive hints about what your talents are and how you can use those talents to contribute. You've ignored the synchronicities and gut feelings your entire life.

"You'll know you are on the right path when you feel joy or inspiration. I repeat because you are somewhat slow to learn. Practice being quiet more and take the time to watch and listen. The signs will appear. Follow the signs to know how you can be of service and connect with those.

Most of all, follow your intuition, particularly in matters of the heart."

Sacha went on to say, "One key is to transcend motivation by looking for inspiration ... which vibrates at a higher frequency than motivation. When you are motivated, you take hold of an idea and focus on achieving objectives, but when you are inspired, the idea takes hold of you in the form of a calling. A right life path is populated with magic moments and guided by synchronous events. Lindsay learned this. When you are following a calling, whether personal or professional, your self-imposed limitations collapse, hibernating talents awaken, and people appear in your life at just the right time.

"It's the vibrational frequency produced by 'inspired' actions ... a high intensity energy field ... that systematically draws other people vibrating at similar frequencies into our lives. They arrive serendipitously."

I understood that inspiration is often inextricably linked with contribution and generosity. Sacha told me, "When you reach a point where generosity becomes your currency, your life will transform ... lighten ... and create a contagion for others to align with. This is the plan B of your soul contract with Lindsay that she wanted you to find!"

Awakening

My meditation was suddenly interrupted by the captain asking the flight attendants to prepare the cabin for landing. As was the case with the insights I'd experienced in Katrina's office, I found the insights from my meditation to be authentic truth.

I'd been living a counterfeit life guided by an uninspiring career ... at least to me ... and a love life highlighted by sport-fucking hot women.

For the first time, I was viewing the world through new eyes. The limited idea of who I was ... Nick Dalton, the miserably unhappy, womanizing investment banker ... had given way to an expanded awareness in which despair was replaced with hope, in which creating a more authentic reality was possible.

From the back of the Midway Airport cab, I used my iPhone to schedule time with Robert on Saturday morning. I'd be resigning my position with Cadwallader Smythe. Financially, it would be a total disaster for me, but at this moment, I'd never felt freer or more deeply into truth.

The Thermster IPO was certain to collapse, no matter how much Doug Rogan and Robert Grimes wanted it to happen. Cadwallader Smythe would survive as a firm, although the partners would take a terrible financial hit.

I directed the cab to Janice's apartment building in Lincoln Park. I'd be ending our toxic eighteen-month escapade tonight ... not that she'd care much. I'd barely heard from her in over a week.

I sent Katrina a text:

> *Awakened. No further sessions necessary. Mere words cannot express my thanks.*

I knew this to be an insufficient thank you and would give further thought on how to properly tell Katrina how thankful I was for all she had done for me. Like an ocean oyster, she's transformed a sorry grain of sand into a humble pearl.

I took a deep breath and smiled from ear to ear for the first time in months. Freedom ... freedom from the need to accumulate things ... freedom from the addiction to meaningless sex.

I had no idea what the next chapter of my life entailed, but I knew it involved living a life shaped by inspiration rather than accumulation ... contribution rather than achievement ... oneness rather than individuality ... and love rather than fear.

Lastly, I penned a short note to Lindsay on the back of the picture Cheryl had given me ... hoping she could somehow see the contents.

Awakening

Dear Lindsay (my one and only),

You saved me from a Soul-Eating Darkness. It was your sunshine that lit the pathway to my awakening. I now know why our souls cautiously approached each other in Ann Arbor. For that one shining moment, your dreams were my dreams, your fears were my fears, and your love was my love. Our journey together in this life has ended, but many more adventures await us ... together. I won't let you down next time. I love you always.

Your Soul Mate,

Nick

A New Beginning

Many, many years after Nick's awakening … It's my first day of fourth grade, a perfect summer day in Sydney, Australia. Hope fills the air as mothers drop off their children at the front of the elementary school. Buses ride in like products off an assembly line. The smell of new paint fills the hallways. The disappointment of a summer break just ended is overwhelmed by the newfound optimism of the dawning school year.

As I entered the school, I said to myself, fourth grade is going to be different. Throughout third grade, I had been one of the kids always picked last for teams, no matter the game. Each day at lunch had been a desperate attempt to find someone to sit with. Often, I found myself eating alone, trying to appear completely anonymous and hoping no one would notice I was sitting alone … again. Day after day, the same drama unfolded. Sometimes I would find a group or single to eat with, but nothing steady. My natural tendency for shyness had smothered my weak attempts to make friends.

This year is going to be different I reiterated as I sat down in my homeroom for the first day of class. While studying the room, I'm noticing most everyone seems to know everyone else … except me. I'm looking everywhere for a friendly face, but no one is reciprocating a smile back at me.

By the time our afternoon recess starts, I'm already repeating last year. I ate alone at lunch, just trying to blend in, all the while, obsessing that everyone who looks my way assumes I'm too big a loser to have friends. Of course, in reality, no one really notices nor cares.

At recess, another humiliation follows as I'm not picked for nine-on-nine kickball. A group of us form and two alpha-males assign themselves as captains and start picking players, alternating one pick each, until eighteen of twenty-one kids are selected. Three of us are left to aimlessly wander the playground looking for something to do.

I stroll over to an unoccupied swing set and sit on one of the swings to watch the kickball game. I grab the swings chains, which are coated in yellow rubber and lift myself onto the padded black seat that conforms to my behind. As my boney, school-uniformed legs dangle a few inches off the ground, I stare longingly at the other kids, listening to them laugh and yell, slowly building lightly formed bonds with each other. I sit and watch anonymously from afar, creating no memories, just trying to get through the day.

As I scan the playground, I look for any other kids who are alone. I notice a tall lanky girl with short blonde hair and glasses struggling to climb up the dome, an interconnected maze of industrial-strength plastic pipes arranged perfectly for climbing and hanging. On a corner of the blacktop adjacent to the playground, an Asian kid is playing tic tac toe with himself and a box of white chalk. In the grass, a girl with a long ponytail is lying flat on her back, staring up at the sky, seemingly talking to herself.

A short girl with shoulder-length brown hair runs up from behind to join me on the swing set. Her hair is in pigtails, each one tied with a bright pink ribbon. She is out of breath, her face beet red, sweat dripping down from her left temple. Looking out the corner of my eye, I see her grab the swing next to me. She is on her tippy toes, trying to back-jump onto the padded black seat. After two unsuccessful attempts to get on the seat, she turns to me. I'm still looking away but trying to see her in my peripheral vision.

With a beaming smile, she says, "Hi, my name is Nicole ... Nicole Stuart. Can you help me get on the swing? I'm a shorty."

"My ... my name's Jacoby Owens. I ... I like your smile. It's pretty," I say, still nervously sitting on my swing. I'm surprised by what has just come out of my mouth, as if the words don't belong to me.

Without saying a word, she shoots me a mischievous glance, looking right into my eyes. She then darts her eyes toward the swing and then back at me, reminding me of her need for help.

She's wearing the largest grin I've ever seen. I jump off my swing and face her directly, hugging my hands around her hips. In one smooth backward jump and lift, Nicole is comfortably on the swing.

She starts kicking her little legs back and forth to create swinging momentum. I climb back onto my swing and start swinging alongside her, in perfect rhythm. Back and forth we swing, seeing how high we each can go.

We continue to swing in perfect unison, both of us making minor kick adjustments to ensure the solidarity of our rhythm. No words are said, although playful fourth-grade giggles are numerous.

Seemingly from nowhere, Nicole trumpets out a hearty, "Hey." Once she is sure she's caught my eye, Nicole looks at me as we swing in perfect unison and says, "I like you, Jacoby Owens."

"I like you too, Nicole Stuart. I've got a good feeling about you."

--END—

"Real love stories never have endings."
                            Unknown